Weird Wedding at Wonky Inn

Wonky Inn Book 3

JEANNIE WYCHERLEY

Weird Wedding at Wonky Inn
Wonky Inn Book 3
BY
JEANNIE WYCHERLEY

Copyright © 2018 Jeannie Wycherley
Bark at the Moon Books
All rights reserved

Publishers note: This is a work of fiction. All characters, names, places and incidents are either products of the author's imagination or are used fictitiously and for effect or are used with permission.

Any other resemblance to actual persons, either living or dead, is entirely coincidental.

No part of this book may be reproduced, distributed or transmitted in any form or by any means, including photocopying, recording, or other electronic or mechanical methods, or by any information storage and retrieval system without the prior written permission of the publisher, except in the case of very brief quotations embodied in critical reviews and certain other non-commercial uses permitted by copyright law.

Sign up for Jeannie's newsletter: http://eepurl.com/cN3Q6L

Weird Wedding at Wonky Inn was edited by Anna Bloom @ The Indie Hub

Cover design by JC Clarke of The Graphics Shed.

*This book is dedicated to
Heaven Riendeau*

Thanks for providing inspiration!

*and to the real Marc Williams
Ditto!*

CONTENTS

Chapter 1	1
Chapter 2	13
Chapter 3	23
Chapter 4	33
Chapter 5	45
Chapter 6	57
Chapter 7	73
Chapter 8	83
Chapter 9	95
Chapter 10	109
Chapter 11	121
Chapter 12	129
Chapter 13	145
Chapter 14	157
Chapter 15	171
Chapter 16	189
Chapter 17	201
Chapter 18	213
Chapter 19	239
Epilogue	259

Acknowledgments	265
Wonky Continues	267
Add Some Magickal Sparkle	269
The Birth of Wonky	271
Please?	273
The Wonky Inn Series	275
Also by Jeannie Wycherley	277
Coming Soon	279

CHAPTER ONE

I'm not sure what first alerted me to the fact I'd found my second corpse in less than six months.

It might have been the faintest whiff of something a little meaty floating towards me on the early autumn breeze. Or, it could have been the stony silence emanating from the cottage in front of me. The sweet little building, so still under the balmy autumn sun, appeared to be holding its breath, waiting.

The day had started wonderfully. I'd taken delivery of one hundred beautifully printed invitations and ventured out to deliver them. Pausing on the front step of my wonky inn, I'd breathed deeply, allowing the fresh air to fill my lungs. Unusually glorious weather for the time of year bathed the grounds of the inn in autumnal sunshine, the sun shone from a brilliant blue sky, the air warmer than you'd generally expect in October in the south-west of England.

Having abandoned my jacket at home, I now strolled from door to door around the village of Whittlecombe to personally invite the local inhabitants to the grand re-opening of Whittle Inn on the 31st October.

Halloween.

Well why not?

With the help of the Wonky Inn Clean-up Crew and together with my great grandmother and namesake, Alfhild Gwynfyre Daemonne—quietly referred to as Gwyn by me—everything was spick and span, freshly painted, and shining like a new pin. There were still some—actually many—last minute touches to attend to, but at last here I was, just a fortnight away from all I had dreamed of since first inheriting the inn from my late mother earlier in the year.

Whittlecombe is a small village. Throughout the wider area we had a population of approximately two hundred and fifty people, but within the actual village itself, there are probably less than forty houses. Twelve of those are cottages tied to my inherited estate, along with the general stores, the café and the post office.

As you'd expect the residents were comprised of

a mix of folk: families, older retired couples, and people living alone. I'd either met or knew most of them by sight, thanks to my regular forays to Whittle Stores and the post office, and of course, invitations to events held in the village hall. I recognised that some of the locals thought of me as a bit of an oddball but given that the inn had been in the Daemonne family for centuries, and we had always been witches, I guessed they were used to it by now.

It was my intention to ensure that the re-opening of Whittle Inn was a community occasion, something that everyone could enjoy. To that end, I was organising a party on the evening of the 31st for the adults in town to join me, if they so wished, for drinks and nibbles and a bit of music from my resident band of ghost minstrels, the Devonshire Fellows.

Luppitt Smeatharpe could hardly contain himself he was so excited. Gone was the sobbing spirit whose tears had ripped my heart asunder only a few weeks before, and in his place, a joyous and talented musician, who filled the inn with subtle harmony and happy Elizabethan dance music.

Well, usually.

To be honest it could get a bit much if I had work to do, or needed to concentrate, and the repetitive beats of Napier's drum seemed to drive Gwyn slightly crazy, but then again, I suspect Gwyn was actually already a little crazy. Nonetheless, I'd set boundaries in place for Luppitt and his friends, and told them they could only rehearse between 10 am and 7 pm. Outside of those times they needed to take themselves into the centre of Speckled Wood, well away from civilization.

The thought of my forthcoming party had me feeling a little thrilled myself. Re-launching the inn was a big deal for me, and simultaneously my heart skipped, and my stomach rolled. I really couldn't wait to get all dressed up and play 'hostess with the mostest', but at the same time I couldn't help worrying that nobody would attend my party and the inn would open to the sound of silence.

No party can ever be complete without the perfect mix of guests, and to that end I was hoping to have plenty of locals attending, so we could all get to know each other better, and they could feel proud of the vital role the village had played in the long history of the inn.

And that's what brought me to Whittle Lane, and my dozen terraced cottages, painted in pastels and lined up like pretty maids all in a row. My friend Millicent Ballicott, a witch in her sixties, lived a few doors up, in Hedge Cottage with her dog Jasper, and I knew the inside of her home quite well. All twelve cottages dated from the early eighteenth century and were small—basically two up and two down—although these days all of them now had a bathroom extension behind the kitchen where the coal store and outside lavatory would once have been, and a few had a double storey extension.

Number 8, or Primrose Cottage as it was called, was in dire need of a lick of external paint, and new windows. I knew from a previous visit, when I'd gone along to introduce myself as his new landlord, that it belonged to an old gentleman by the name of Derek Pearce. He had struck me as a quiet man, not given to socialising much, but he had seemed pleasant enough. He kept the inside of his cottage clean and neat and as I'd explained to him when we'd met, I fully intended to refresh the outside of the cottage the following spring. The inn had taken much of my time, attention and finances, but now that we were ready to open, I could start planning to take care of my other responsibilities.

As with the other cottages on Whittle Lane, Primrose Cottage had a tiny iron front gate that came up to mid-thigh on me, and then a small patch of walled front garden. Derek had planted several rose bushes in his patch, and although they needed a prune, the late blooming roses in yellow and peach were a joy to behold. Their fresh subtle scent caused me to pause and enjoy the moment.

Hard to believe that just six months previously, I'd been choked daily by car and Tube fumes in the smog of London, while commuting with millions of other people, many of whom seemed to have sprayed themselves liberally in expensive but synthetic perfumes and colognes. Nothing you could buy over the counter smelled as heady as the countryside after a sharp shower of rain in my opinion. I had fallen in love with the countryside in a way I had never imagined I would.

So, taking the moment for myself, I bent my head to the roses and took a deep sniff, and that's when I caught the tiniest whiff of something not quite right.

Not being able to place the smell, and not being overly concerned in any case, I took the few steps to the front door, tucked under a pretty gable, and reached out to knock.

The door opened a crack as my knuckles met the wood.

"Hello Mr Pearce?" I called.

No reply.

"Mr Pearce?" I repeated, more loudly. Some of

the older tenants in these houses could be a little hard of hearing, and some struggled to see.

This time when there was still no response, I swung the door open a little more. There was every chance the old man was perfectly alright, and I didn't need to feel concerned. Perhaps he was in the back garden hanging out his washing or tending to his begonias, who knew? Maybe he had left the door open by mistake. But there was always the '*what if?*' What if he had fallen and needed help? What if he had drowned in the bath?

While I didn't like to go inside unannounced, I figured it would be wise to check on him.

Feeling rather like an intruder, and with guilt sitting heavily in the pit of my stomach, I tip-toed quietly into the front room, grimacing at the idea I was trespassing. Everything seemed to be in order, and I was about to call out again, when I heard the faintest of whimpers coming from behind a closed wooden door.

Clutching my pile of undelivered invitations, I scampered over and pulled the door towards me, expecting to find a cupboard, but instead discovering the entrance to the narrow uneven stairs up to the first floor. A small Yorkshire Terrier dog stood on the first landing, where the stairs turned out of view, shivering with fear, its ears flat and pulled pack, panting hard.

"Hello, sweetheart," I crooned. "What's the matter?" With my free hand, I reached out towards the tiny animal, but it shrank away from me. I pulled my hand back, startled.

"It's okay, baby," I said, keeping my voice low and calm. "You're alright. No-one is going to hurt you."

I climbed the first step, talking quietly, and then another. "Where's your Dad? Is he up here?" I wanted to call out to Mr Pearce once more, but I was worried that I would scare the dog again, so I inched towards it, crouching over to make myself smaller, soothing it with quiet words, until I could have bent down and scooped it up.

From around the corner of the landing and to my right, there came a buzzing noise, much like I'd expect an angry hornet to make, rapidly followed by a loud clattering. This would be the direction of the front bedroom presumably. The dog yelped and shot past me, jumping down the stairs and hightailing it through the open door at the bottom. I turned, meaning to go after it and ensure it was safe, but the clattering came again, and the buzzing seemed louder and more insistent.

Scarcely daring to breathe, I took the last three stairs in quick time, then paused, inching my head to peer around the corner, frightened of what I would see. The bedroom door stood ajar. Mr Pearce lay sprawled on the floor next to his perfectly made bed, one hand outstretched, a few feet away from my own location.

He wasn't moving.

That was bad enough.

But lifting my eyes away from the old man, I took a second to focus on something bobbing around in the air at shoulder height.

A small red globe, threaded with gold.

No larger than a cricket ball, it spun round and around, throwing gold glitter in the air and buzzing with angry intent. The same instant I understood exactly what I was seeing, it launched itself at me.

I ducked and screamed at the same time, scattering my invitations all over the floor, to taken aback to cast a spell to protect myself. It flew around me in a circle, as quick as a flash, and as I gazed up at it in horror, it hovered in front of my face, inches away from my eyes. Then with a final angry zipping noise it launched itself at the closed bedroom window and catapulted itself through, smashing a hole as it went, the glass splintering like a spider's web. By the time

I'd clambered back to my feet and dashed to the window, it had gone.

The Mori.

I had hoped we—Wizard Shadowmender and his friends who had turned out to help me—had vanquished them during the Battle of Speckled Wood, but I think in my heart of hearts I had always known we hadn't run them off for good.

Now I stood at the window, perplexed by what I could see, and examined the almost perfectly spherical hole in the glass, before remembering the man on the floor. I turned back to Mr Pearce.

It was too late for the old man. He lay on his back, his head cocked at an awkward angle, and his eyes wide open. It might have been my imagination, but his features appeared fixed in an expression of dread. Tentatively, I reached out trembling fingers to touch him. Cold.

I pulled my hand back with a gasp of dismay.

He'd been gone a while.

I knew better than to touch anything else.

With my eyes darting left and right, worried that there might be other threats from The Mori around, I slid quickly down the stairs, intent on my making my way back out onto Whittle Lane and the salvation of Millicent Ballicott's cottage just a few doors down, but the whimpering of the Yorkshire Terrier halted me in my tracks. I couldn't leave it here; the poor thing was as petrified as me.

Following its cries, I found it cowering by the back door. I scooped it up and hugged it to my chest, then in double-quick time ran back through the cottage and the front garden. This time, the thorns from the rose bushes reached out with malevolence to scratch at me.

Seconds later I was banging on Millicent's door and without waiting for a response, bursting in on the sanctity of her front room.

CHAPTER TWO

"So what aren't you telling me?" DS George Gilchrist fixed me with his all-knowing blue eyes and stared at me with piercing intensity.

I tried to avoid his gaze, but sitting knee to knee, across from each other at the mini-dining table, in Millicent's miniscule kitchen, I really didn't have many options.

I shrugged. "It's pretty much how I told you. I was delivering the invitations. The door was open. I went in. I heard the little dog crying, and when I investigated I found poor Mr Pearce upstairs." I shuddered, remembering his face.

Gilchrist raised his eyebrows. "Yes that's what you said." He waited for me to continue and when I didn't, he stood, and quietly closed the kitchen door, shutting Millicent—who was currently comforting the Yorkshire Terrier while Jasper, her lurcher, looked on impassively—out from our conversation.

He returned and took his seat, taking my clammy hand in his dry one. "How's your arm?" he asked.

"It's much better, you know it is." I smiled, his touch warming me through. Since the incident at the inn, when I'd been attacked by Martin Toynbee, George had been keeping tabs on me. We'd even been out for drinks and dinner once or twice, and to the cinema too. I was enjoying his company.

"Good."

He squeezed my hand and I looked across at his handsome face, his eyes soft, his mouth curled in a gentle smile.

"You don't think Derek Pearce died of natural causes, do you?" I asked, keeping my expression neutral.

George shook his head. "No. I have to be honest, I don't. Now, my colleague out there," he cocked his head in the direction of the Pearce cottage, "is working on the theory that something came through the window, maybe a cricket ball or something of that size, and the shock caused Mr Pearce to fall and suffer a head injury. Perhaps a broken neck." George narrowed his eyes at me. "That's his thinking. It's not mine."

"What's yours?" I asked, attempting a light tone.

"Whatever broke that window did so when it exited the cottage, not when it entered. It's basic police work. The glass is on the outside. The velocity of the object caused the glass to fall outwards as it burst through the glass."

"Okay." I swallowed.

"So am I supposed to assume that Mr Pearce threw a cricket ball through the window in the seconds before he died?" George's expression darkened. He didn't like to be taken for a fool. "I don't think so."

"That doesn't seem likely, I agree," I said and the DS's face fell.

"You know more than you're letting on."

"George—" I began.

"I know you're a witch. I've accepted that, haven't I?" He waved jazz hands at me, palm up. "You told me all about the ghosts. I've met a few, including Gwyn—"

"You lucky man."

"She's not that bad," George protested in her defence. I rolled my eyes. For some reason my great grandmother, Gwyn, and George, were getting on very well. "I believed you, didn't I?"

I had to give him that. "Yes, you did."

"So give me the benefit of the doubt. Why not tell me the whole story of what went on in that cottage earlier? Were there more ghosts?"

I sat back in my chair and scowled. "If I tell you, you may believe me, but nobody else will. Your superiors will think you're barking."

"But I can't do my job unless I know the whole truth, Alf. You need to help me out."

I understood his predicament fully. I also knew there was no way The Mori would ever be stopped by any common mortal. George wasn't going to let it drop however. I suppose you don't get to be a Detective Sergeant if you roll over at the first sign of an obstacle, do you? In this case, I was the obstacle.

I sighed. "When we first met you may remember I had a chap in helping with the painting and decorating at the inn."

"Oh yes. I'd forgotten about him," George replied, his tone casual. There was no way George had forgotten about Jed. "You two seemed pretty close at the time if I remember correctly."

"We were close." I nodded. *I'd thought we were in love. More fool me.* "He turned out to be a member of an organization known as The Mori."

"The Mori?"

"They're an international organization, highly

secretive. Made up almost entirely of warlocks, but supported in their endeavours by mortals." I clarified, "Ordinary folk with poor intentions."

"And what are their endeavours?"

"Probably to make as much capital as possible, but they're anti-environmental, so they make their money by selling green spaces to property developers."

"There's a lot of money in property."

"Too much." I nodded, pinching my lips together.

"What's the difference between a warlock and a witch?" George asked, his brow furrowed as he tried to get his head around the content of the conversation. "Is a warlock a male witch?"

"Kind of. Sometimes. Warlock is a harsh term and one that should never be clumsily bandied about. Many of our kind find it offensive. Witches can be male or female, they're simply practitioners of magick. But warlock comes from the Old English word wærloga, which means a traitor, or a liar or oath-breaker. In this case, the warlocks in The Mori —all male as far as I know—have been banished from whichever coven they belonged to, for wrongdoings of some description."

"There are no women in The Mori?"

"Apparently not. But it's a highly secretive organisation, and no-one can really be sure who belongs to it."

George nodded. "And your painter and decorator friend was a member of this organization?"

"His name was Jed," I said, my tone curt. I didn't like to think of him and the way he had betrayed me. "He—and his friends—were intent on ruining the inn, making the business fail, so that they could buy my land cheaply. They were particularly interested in the wood I own out the back of the inn. Then their intention was to sell it on to a local landowner, so he could build a housing estate."

"And you foiled him." It was a statement not a question.

George reached across to stroke my arm and I realised how uptight I must appear with my shoulders scrunched up under my head, my arms folded defensively across my chest and my eyes screwed up with loathing.

I breathed deeply. "Yes. You're right. I did." I rolled my shoulders back, trying to relax.

"But you think The Mori are back?"

"I know they are." I jerked forwards once more. "When I went up into Mr Pearce's bedroom I saw one of them. They take the form of a …" I cast about looking for the right words to use to explain what I meant. "A spinning globe is the best way I can describe it." I made a small round shape with my hands. "In this case it was the size of a tennis ball or a cricket ball or something like that. They can be bigger. Much bigger. Each globe looks like a Christmas bauble that you would hang on a tree. Red, with a gold thread running through it. They float in the air, spinning really quickly."

George regarded me quizzically, but I pushed on.

"These baubles, or globes, or orbs, or whatever you want to call them, they attract energy. Negative energy. They use the energy to grow."

"And one of these killed Mr Pearce?"

"I didn't see that. I had the sense that Mr Pearce had been lying there for some time before I found him."

"The pathologist on scene reckons he's been dead for over 48 hours."

I grimaced. "So that globe had been there with the body all that time? I wonder why?"

"Do you think that's what killed him?" George asked. "Can these globe things kill?"

I thought back to the Battle of Speckled Wood. "Yes. I've seen them grow to the size of a small car, like a mini or something. The Mori use these orbs as carriers, like a form of transport. I saw one transform into Jed. But the spinning orbs aren't harmless, by any means. They can shoot energy beams. Yes. They can kill."

"Hmm," George took a few notes.

I watched him as he processed all I'd told him. When he looked at me again, I could see the questions in his eyes, so I asked them for him.

"What did The Mori want with Mr Pearce? And why did they leave him dead?"

"So what will happen now?" I asked George as I walked him back to Primrose Cottage. He slipped under the blue and white tape and turned to face me. His frown told me he wasn't sure.

"I'll have to help continue to process the scene and pursue various lines of enquiry as my colleagues see fit."

"But—"

"But, given what you've told me, I'll keep my eyes peeled and I'll be asking a lot of questions," he replied firmly. "You're right. No-one else will believe what you've shared with me. Let's keep it between ourselves, alright?" He raised his voice as a uniformed officer came our way. "That's all I can tell you for now, Ms Daemonne."

I nodded. "That's good enough," I said, and smiled, although my lips felt thin and dry and stiff.

He glanced behind him at the open door. Beyond, I could see a few shadows moving around. "I'll see if I can gather up your invitations and let you have them back."

"Yes. Thanks. I suppose I need to finish my rounds in the village. Just drop them at the shop if you like."

"Will do. Is there one for me?"

"There might be." I smirked.

"When we first met you promised me you'd invite me to the opening of the inn."

He had a good memory. "So I did, DS Gilchrist. Although I thought it might be in a working capacity rather than a personal one."

"Did you?" he asked, his voice low. He leaned forwards, across the tape, and my heart skipped a beat thinking he would kiss me, but he stopped, inches away from my face, as though remembering he was on duty and in public. Instead he pulled back and smiled at me. "Don't worry. We'll get to the bottom of it."

"Just be careful," I said, and realised with a jolt that him staying safe was more important to me than I might previously have cared to admit. "The Mori are deadly."

"I will," he said and with one last lingering look, he turned away and entered the cottage. I heard someone call him and then the door closed, leaving me on the narrow pavement alone, shivering despite the relatively warm afternoon.

Chapter Three

Whittle General Stores, run by my friends Rhona and Stan, had long been the centre of the community. Today was no exception. People were gathering both inside and outside to discuss the goings on down Whittle Lane. Those loitering outside could just about make out the police cordon, and of course there were numerous marked police cars and vans parked on the road. Whittlecombe being such a small village meant everybody tended to know what was going on immediately, and as they say, good news travels fast, but bad news travels faster still.

"Poor Mr Pearce," I overheard, as I made my way up the path to the shop entrance.

"Oh it's a tragedy. Lived in the village his whole life, you know," said a second bystander.

"He's never been the same man since his wife passed away though. In some ways, this will be a welcome release," the first voice said and there were murmurs among the throng of people. I couldn't tell if they were in acquiescence or disagreement with this turn of thought, so I kept my head down and doggedly continued along my trajectory, not wishing to answer any questions about my role in finding him.

Rhona and Stan were both busy serving customers, so I hid my face at the newspaper stand and waited for a lull in proceedings. It took a while. Everyone had something to say about Derek Pearce, and understandably they wanted to share their memories.

I listened in to their conversations with half an ear.

Despite having lived in the village his whole life, in excess of sixty years, it seemed that for the past five or six he had become increasingly reclusive. His wife had died prematurely, I couldn't glean why, and he had folded into himself, spurning invitations and spending most of his time on his allotment.

I knew all about the allotments. They were on a patch of land belonging to my Whittle Inn estate, and were available to anyone who paid rent on one of my tied cottages. Most of the cottages had only small gardens, many without even a hint of lawn, and so the allotments were a wonderful way for the tenants to grow fruit, vegetables and even flowers if they desired.

Other than that, people didn't seem to know very much about him. He had no children and no other close family.

Just his little dog, I thought. Such a sad and quiet existence

I flicked absently though the magazines, not taking in the content on the pages at all, until Rhona's voice broke into my thoughts, making me jump.

"Alf?"

"Sorry," I said, turning my attention to the couple behind the counter. "I was miles away."

"I heard you discovered poor Mr Pearce. How terrible for you."

"I was delivering invitations to the grand opening of the inn," I explained. "In fact, that's what I've popped in for. I dropped them in the cottage, and George... ah... DS Gilchrist is going to bring them here and leave them for me once the police have finished up in there."

Rhona nodded. "I'll save them for you. Perhaps Stan can finish delivering them for you?"

Stan smiled at his wife. He was a quiet, perfectly unassuming man. His wife was fond of finding extra jobs to keep him busy.

"Oh there's no need, thank you. I'm happy to deliver them personally." My voice caught in my throat and embarrassed I looked away, but not before Rhona spotted how upset I was.

"Oh you poor love," she cried, squeezing out from behind her counter. Stan subtly melted through to the back of the shop, thoughtfully making himself scarce while I behaved in a decidedly un-British way, thereby sparing my blushes. "It must have been a shock for you." She wrapped me in a supportive embrace. "What a few months you're having! I promise, it's not all doom and gloom like this in Whittlecombe normally."

"Only since I arrived here, you mean?" I asked, blinking rapidly. We looked at each other and burst into laughter, me through my tears.

"Just a coincidence, I'm sure," Rhona giggled. She broke off as another customer walked in. I recognised her as a waitress at The Hay Loft, the other hostelry in town, main rival to my wonky inn. When I'd first met her, her hair had been dyed red, now it had been bleached blonde. It looked more normal, but not as interesting.

Situated just across the road from the General Stores, I found The Hay Loft, altogether too modern and bland, and was determined that Whittle Inn would serve an entirely different clientele altogether.

The more supernatural kind.

"Hey, Charity," Rhona greeted the young woman, and Charity smiled.

"Hi Rhona. How are you doing?" She glanced at me curiously, obviously noting my tears but politely refrained from acknowledging them.

"Very well," Rhona said and with one last squeeze of my shoulder resumed her place behind the counter. "Although it's a very sad day for Whittlecombe."

"Yes it is." Charity nodded, her face grave. "Poor Mr Pearce. I didn't know him very well, although I've lived next-door-but-one to him my whole life, but it's still incredibly sad."

Of course. I had forgotten. Charity and her mother lived at Snow Cottage.

"I saw him out walking Sunny last night. It was all so sudden," Charity added, and I turned towards her, no longer concerned with my tear-stained face.

"Last night?" I blurted. "That's impossible."

Charity glanced at me sharply. "What do you mean?"

Hadn't George mentioned the pathologist was assuming Mr Pearce had been dead for over two days? I was sure that's what he'd said. Perhaps it was better not to repeat such information though. I shrugged, sinking into a wave of misery. "Ignore me," I said, but I could see that Charity had put two and two together.

Her face flushed. "Oh."

We exchanged glances. I had the feeling Charity had more she wanted to say to me, but wouldn't in front of Rhona.

"I need to get back to the inn," I said. "Sorry for crying on you, Rhona."

"Oh don't worry, pet. That's what friends are for." She smiled. "I'll hold on to your invitations when DS Gilchrist drops them in."

"Thanks. I appreciate it." Nodding at Charity, I made my way out of the shop and headed a little way down the road in the direction of the inn, walking slowly up Whittle Lane, out of the village.

It wasn't long before I heard the patter of footsteps running after me and I turned as Charity slid to a stop.

Before she could open her mouth, I said, "You see ghosts."

She looked me straight in the eye. "I do."

We meandered along the road. Charity offered me one of the soft mints she'd purchased from Rhona and I chewed thoughtfully while she told me her story.

"I've always been able to see them. I've never known my father. It's always been just me and my mum. When she found out she was pregnant with me, Mum was living in Manchester. She moved back down here and in with her mum, my grandmother Ivy." Charity laughed. "She was a case, Ivy. Into everything. Clubs and societies, and organising fetes and events. She loved it. And everyone in Whittlecombe loved her."

Charity offered me another mint and I took one. They were refreshing in a sweet treat kind of way.

"Ivy died when I was 8 and right from the word go I could still see her. She'd come and read me stories when I went to bed. At her funeral, people told me not to be sad, but I wasn't sad. She was still with me."

"And is she still with you?" I asked, looking around for any tell-tale ghost light that might indicate a spirit's presence.

"From time to time yes, but mainly in the cottage. I don't see her out and about anymore." Charity watched me glancing about, curiosity written on her face. "Can you see ghosts too?"

"Yes. More than I'd like sometimes."

"Does it run in your family?" Charity asked. "Only, everyone knows that you folk up there at the old inn have a rather unusual history. My Mum always calls you the Adams Family."

"Does she?" I asked, unsure whether to be affronted or not. In the end however, I giggled. "Better than the Munsters, I suppose."

"You're a part of Whittlecombe's history," Charity continued. "A part of what makes all of us who live in the village, the people that we are."

"That's a lovely thing to say." I'd never thought of our family being seen that way.

Charity smiled. She was so warm, and her face so open. No wonder she was good at what she did. She'd certainly made her mark on me when I first met her at The Hay Loft.

A sudden thought occurred to me. "Do you like working at The Hay Loft?"

Charity shrugged. "It pays the bills. But they made me dye my hair to a more natural colour."

I nodded, pondering on what to do. It probably wasn't ethical to try and poach staff from your main rival, but I knew Charity was good at what she did. My long experience of the hospitality industry in London had taught me that good staff were hard to come by. In fact, hadn't I recently tried and failed to find a decent chef for the inn?

"That's a shame," I said. We reached Charity's cottage and I paused by her gate. We dropped our heads, as two doors away, a covered gurney was brought out from Primrose Cottage, carrying poor Derek Pearce's body.

We stood quietly and respectfully, while the old man was loaded into the back of the ambulance, and watched as it drove slowly away, heading for the morgue and a post-mortem in Exeter no doubt.

My insides quivered like jelly. "Life can be cruel sometimes."

"And incredibly short," Charity agreed. "He was only in his mid-sixties."

I sighed. "Indeed."

I was about to say my goodbyes and continue up the road, when Charity chimed in again. "That's food for thought, isn't it? I mean, that life is so short?"

She gestured behind her, back into the village. "I don't really like working at The Hay Loft if I'm honest. Lyle is a big pain in the neck."

I smiled.

"So if you were thinking of offering me a job…?"

"Come up and see me," I replied. "I'm definitely hiring."

Chapter Four

To say I was a little pre-occupied when Charity arrived at the inn the next morning after her breakfast shift at The Hay Loft is something of an understatement.

I'd been looking forward to the opening of the inn very much, and so far I'd accepted a few bookings, but I fully intended to have a 'soft' opening, meaning I'd trial the inn on a few guests to check that all the hospitality the guests needed, and all the systems I needed, were fully functional. My plan was then to gradually step up to full occupancy once we were in the swing of things. But now I'd had a letter from a potential client going by the name of Sabien Laurent, enquiring whether he could hire out all available rooms in order to host a wedding for his son, Melchior.

He appreciated that it was rather last-minute,

but he'd been let down by a well-known hotel in London, and someone—he didn't specify who—had suggested he try me at Whittle Inn.

For some reason I couldn't help but be suspicious. I poured over the letter, written in red ink on fine quality parchment, in an old-fashioned cursive hand. I scrutinised the writing, and read the words over and over, searching for details, trying to read between the lines. No matter how I inspected the letter I found no clues as to who Sabien was, or whether I had grounds for my unease. I felt sorely tempted to write back with a resounding 'no', after all, I'd made my plans for my grand opening. And yet...

And yet, I wanted to get Whittle Inn on the map. I needed guests. Surely this would be the best way to go about that.

Zephaniah, my ghost-of-all-trades, showed Charity up to my office, and I hurriedly stuffed the letter under a few others on my desk. As Zephaniah took his leave, I watched her reaction to him. She did a double take. "Wow," she said. "Is he for real?"

"Hi!" I laughed, happy to see her. "He's a useful ghost to have around. You'll love him." I worried how she would react to the inn, and the ghosts, especially after working in The Hay Loft with all its mod cons.

But nothing ventured, nothing gained, and I had a good feeling about this. "Let me show you around."

Charity's eyes were like saucers. "My Mum's right. You *are* the modern equivalent of the Adams Family," she whispered. "This place is amazing. So wonderfully gothic."

"Well thank you, I think."

"It's amazing," she repeated. "You've done a lot of work on it recently, I'm guessing? Everything smells so clean and fresh…"

"And newly painted?" I laughed. "Practically everything has been rubbed down, re-painted or redecorated. A few walls knocked down here and there. Plumbing in some of the bathrooms. New en-suites in fact. New flooring in places. Tiling. Fittings and fixtures. Bedding, beds, curtains and rugs. Even replacement windows in some rooms."

"So just the finishing touches to do?" Charity gestured at the empty walls. "A little dressing to make the place look homely?"

"Yes. I haven't made any final decisions about that, but you're right. I've been slacking. There are so many things to think about." I led her back downstairs and through into the bar room. I'd had the wooden floor boards sanded and varnished, and then I'd covered a large section of the floor with an enormous and beautiful oriental rug in reds, rust, brown and cream. There were several high-backed arm chairs recovered in red velvet and a mix and match of chairs and tables, all lovingly restored by my Wonky Inn Ghostly Clean-up crew. They'd done a grand job.

A large fire burned merrily in the enormous fireplace, and the bar was now almost fully stocked with wines, mixers and spirits. I was awaiting a delivery of barrels to the cellar, so that we could channel real ales, beer and cider to the pumps and have local brews on tap.

Florence, my smouldering house maid ghost, was busily dusting the colourful optics. She shot a look of alarm my way as I entered with Charity. I held my hand up to stop her from bolting at the sight of the newcomer.

"Charity, this is Florence. She was a house maid here at the inn in my great grandmother's time. She's an invaluable member of my team."

Charity scanned Florence from head to toe and gawped at her burning clothes. She took a moment to process what she was seeing before her face lit up. "Pleased to meet you, Florence."

Florence beamed at her in return and dropped a curtsey.

"And you, miss." She turned to me with a cheeky smile. "Nice for you to have a friend, Miss Alf."

"I'm showing Charity around the inn, Florence. She might be interested in working with us, if we're lucky." *If you ghosts all behave this time*.

"I'm liking what I've seen so far," Charity interjected.

"Out the back here." I led Charity through the frosted glass door. "We have The Nook and The Snug. These are small rooms, that can be booked for meetings, or small family gatherings, or we can just allow anybody in here if they need a bit of privacy, I suppose," I said and stood back so Charity could poke her head in.

"Nice," she said, nodding. I'd left both rooms quite plain. Each had a small fireplace, a large table, benches along two of the walls and a few chairs. I'd scattered a bright array of Indian cushions on the benches and hung jewel-coloured silk gauze curtains against the windows, to give a slightly oriental feel. The rooms were pretty and warm.

"Here on the right is the kitchen." We walked through the last door at the end of the corridor, adjacent to the back stairs. "Most of the equipment is left over from before me, but we have a new dishwasher, and a couple of brand-new catering fridges. There's a cold store, pantry and a few storerooms out the back there. All I've really had done in here, is a deep clean and new tiling." The white ceramic tiles, stainless steel work surfaces and cupboard doors gleamed.

"We have a new chef arriving any time. I haven't met him yet."

"You didn't interview him?" Charity asked, raising her eyebrows. I shook my head. "That surprises me. You seem so in control of everything else that's happening."

"Let's just say that I made a bit of a mess of trying to hire a chef, so I had to bow to pressure, and hand the hiring of him or her to my great grandmother."

"Your great grandmother…?"

"Is dead. Yes. She's another ghost who inhabits the inn. I'm sure you'll meet her sooner rather than later. She's an… erm… formidable presence." Charity looked perturbed. "No, look, honestly? She's a pussy-cat." I waved my hands vaguely. "A wolf in a pussy-cat's clothing maybe."

"How many ghosts are there at the inn?"

"Sixty-two usually," I said. "I can be precise because there's not long been an audit." Sometimes I caught myself saying some very odd things, but in this case it was completely true. Perdita Pugh had accounted for sixty-four ghosts, and I'd had two exorcised. "Believe it or not."

Charity nodded, taking it all in her stride. "We have a few that come and go," I continued. "My father is one of those, and we have a band of musicians called The Devonshire Fellows who travel to other places to play, but they've made Whittle Inn their base. For better or for worse, depending on how much you like late medieval wind instruments really. They're currently in residence." I tipped my head, listening intently, but couldn't hear them.

"How lovely," Charity said. "Music on tap, so to speak."

"Mm," I said doubtfully. "It certainly can be."

I threw open the back door. "There's not much to see here. We'll do more work on the grounds starting in the new year. There's a large outdoor storage shed over there where we keep the gardening equipment, wood and coal. There's also a small wood pile just here to the left of the door, so we don't have to traipse to the main shed."

We stood together out the back. I'd found the body of Edvard Zadzinsky here six months ago. That had been my rude awakening to The Mori. So much water had passed under the bridge since then, but the fear of The Mori and what they could do to my inn and grounds had lodged itself deep inside my stomach like a hard stone.

In the distance the trees of Speckled Wood danced gently in a light autumn breeze. I sighed. The wood called to me as always. "So beautiful," I said.

Charity followed my look. "That's part of the estate?"

"Yes, it is. The guests can walk there if they wish." I nearly added, '*it's safe, because I keep it so.*' The wood was locked down tightly with a secure perimeter, magickal workings from my friends, the wizards, Shadowmender and Kephisto. I hiked out there once or twice a week and refreshed the positive energy, always on the lookout for any traces that The Mori had infiltrated my land again.

"And this over here?" Charity gestured towards an area of clear ground.

"There used to be a stable block there. I was going to build a couple of external suites, but unfortunately it burned down."

"You could create a pavilion there. It would be lovely in the summer."

I looked at Charity with admiration. She had plenty of ideas and wasn't afraid to voice them. I liked that about her.

We made our way back upstairs and into my office. I took a seat at my desk and Charity dropped into one of the threadbare armchairs by the fire.

I shuffled the papers on my desk, my eye caught by the letter enquiring about holding the wedding at my inn. I pulled it out and read it again, frowning. What should I do?

"Problem?" asked Charity.

"I'm not sure." I screwed my face up. "I have a potential client who wants to hold his son's wedding here on 31st October."

"The same day you're due to open?"

"Exactly. I think it would be too much. I'm not sure I could cope."

"Of course you could!" Charity exploded with enthusiasm. "It would be the perfect way to open Whittle Inn to the public once more. You said you're getting a new chef, right?"

"Yes."

"Then you can showcase a range of wonderful culinary delights, along with drinks—maybe cocktails—from your newly restocked bar. The inn will never look better than it does right now. Fresh and welcoming."

She had a point.

"All you need is to finish off with some cosy

touches as we were saying, plenty of fresh flowers... that kind of thing. Oh a romantic wedding would be a perfect start for you as the new owner of Whittle Inn. You should go for it!" Her enthusiasm was infectious and as she spoke I found myself imagining a wonderful day with the happy bride and groom, a quiet and sophisticated adult party, the inn dressed to perfection and looking its sparkly best.

"Yes, maybe I should."

"So, do you need a waitress?" she asked. "I mean, you could use your ghosts too, to serve entrees and drinkies. I could train them in silver service if necessary. I always enjoy training new members of staff at The Hay Loft. No member of staff ever stays there very long, so I do it often."

I observed her, sitting in the armchair, leaning towards me with excitement. She had dressed to impress to the best of her means, but money earned from waiting does not stretch very far. She looked smart, although her shoes were cheap and her suit of inferior quality. Her bleached hair was caught in a neat bun at the nape of her neck. The white blouse under her jacket had been washed too often.

But wit and intelligence shone out of her face.

She was entirely wasted as a waitress at The Hay Loft.

"No." I shook my head firmly. "I need more than that. I need someone who can work with me as a Jill-of-all-trades. Someone with common sense and practical abilities. Someone who is neither phased by the spirits inhabiting this inn—particularly my Grandmama—or the rather odd guests I'm sure we're going to attract. I need someone firm but compassionate, open-minded but far-sighted. I need a manager for the inn, Charity. Someone who can step in when I'm not here." I swing back on my chair and grinned at her. "In short, I think you're that person."

Charity shrank back in her seat in surprise, her mouth a wide O. She shook her head in disbelief, examined my face to make sure I was serious and then laughed nervously. "Are you sure?" she asked.

"I am."

"Well, I don't know quite what to say."

"We can try it out for six months and see what you think. I'll be interested in any ideas you have, that will ensure the inn runs smoothly. We can certainly explore the idea of a pavilion for the summer. Anything like that, any ideas you have, just pipe up." Charity, flushed, blew her hair from her face and fanned herself with her hands.

"That's such a vote of confidence, Alf."

"Do you have any questions?" I asked, curious as

to why she wasn't jumping up and down and shrieking "I'll take it!"

"Just one," she said, and drew her long hair out from the scrunchie at the back of neck. "Would you mind if I re-dyed my hair?"

Chapter Five

After Charity had left I looked down at the letter from Sabien Laurent. I would need to reply to him in the affirmative and soon, but first, the growing sensation in my stomach told me I needed to grab a bite to eat.

I skipped down the back stairs feeling more positive than ever that everything to do with Whittle Inn's opening would work out fine. Charity, regardless of the colour of her hair, was going to do me proud. I was sure of it.

With no sign of Florence, it appeared the onus for making lunch was on me. I rummaged in the bread bin and found the knob from a loaf and located cheese in one of the fridges. Cheese on toast was probably the limits of my culinary expertise.

I was on my hands and knees in front of a cupboard under one of the counters, hunting for the cheese grater—without much luck—when the sound of someone clearing their throat behind me, startled me.

"One second," I said. "It must be here somewhere."

"Alfhild?" my great grandmother's unmistakeably imperious tone interrupted me. "I need to introduce you to someone."

I pushed myself to my feet. Beside her was a large rotund man with an impressive moustache and a shining bald head, dressed all in white. It was impossible to miss that he was also slightly transparent and floating about an inch above the floor.

The new chef.

My heart sank.

The new chef was a ghost?

"Now don't pull that face, Alfhild. If the wind changes you'll stay that way," Gwyn barked at me. "Remember your manners. This is Monsieur Emietter. He has come all the way from Paris."

"With all due respect, Grandmama, he's a ghost."

Gwyn affected a shocked face, that might have been quite comic if I hadn't been so taken aback. "You don't say, my dear."

"I was intent on hiring—"

"Someone who didn't like ghosts. *That* would have been rather a catastrophe, Alfhild."

"Not so. Grandmama—"

"Or what about the applicant you interviewed, who tried to have everyone in the building exorcised? I found that little mistake particularly spectacular."

She had me beat. I had tried and failed to find a chef. Now only days from opening, I was hardly in a position to dismiss Gwyn's choice and start a search for a new one.

"Pleased to meet you, Monsieur Emietter," I said, sounding for all the world like a sulky teenager.

"That's better, Alfhild." Gwyn smiled, smug to her transparent core. "But Monsieur Emietter does not speak English."

"Pardon?"

"Not a word."

I rubbed my temples in horror. "Are you serious, Grandmama? How on earth am I going to give him instructions?"

"Well that's where I'll come in, darling. I speak French. You'll have to tell me what you need, and I'll translate it for our new chef."

"Right," I said. Was she for real? She'd probably had this planned all along. A bit of a control freak, my great grandmother.

I smiled at Monsieur Emietter. "Welcome, welcome," I said loudly, as though that would help him to understand, and gestured around at the kitchen. "Make yourself at home. If you need anything just let me—or my bossy grandmother know." I smiled with gritted teeth and stomped out of the kitchen before Gwyn could retort. So intent was I on storming away, I nearly walked straight through Florence as she returned from the bar.

"Ooh," the maid giggled. "That tickles. Everything alright, Miss Alf?"

I pulled up short. "Do you speak any French, Florence?"

"No, miss." Florence looked at me in alarm.

"Ha! Well you're going to have as much fun as me then."

A little later when I'd calmed down, and Florence had delivered a few delicious slices of cheese on toast and a large steaming mug of tea, oh and not forgetting an enormous slice of coffee and walnut cake, I was feeling a little less angst-ridden and slightly more capable of holding an adult conversation with Gwyn.

We sat together in my office while I outlined the plans as they stood for the grand opening of the inn.

"Oh and there's the small matter of the wedding," I said, keeping my tone cavalier.

"What wedding?" Gwyn took the bait straight away. I knew she would. She stared at me with bright shining eyes. At times she reminded me of a mistrustful-looking shrew.

"I've had a letter." I waved the sheet of parchment at her. "A potential customer who would like to hold his son's wedding here on the 31st."

"Of October?"

"Yes."

"That's the same day we open."

"I know. Exciting isn't it?" It was my turn to sound a little smug although to be honest, I was still a tad worried about maxing out the inn's capabilities.

"Well if you think we can cope," Gwyn said, and I eyed her with suspicion. She knew something.

"You've been listening into my conversations again, haven't you?" These blasted ghosts and their abilities to apparate here and there and walk through walls and doors. It could be incredibly inconvenient at times.

Gwyn shrugged, a picture of innocence. "Your young lady visitor, you mean?"

"You know I do," I growled.

"She seemed very nice. Very forthright. What did she mean about dying her hair?"

"It's something young people like to do these days, Grandmama. Well, not just young people actually. Anyone."

"You've hired her, I hope?"

Now it was my turn to be surprised. "You approve?"

"We could do with someone with a little nous around here."

"Nowse? Is that French?"

"Oh I do beg your pardon, darling." She laughed, a tinkling sound. Not a sound I heard emanating from my stern and solemn great grandmother very often. I knew she was taking the mickey out of me for not speaking any modern languages. "No not French. It means common sense, you know, practical intelligence…"

I figured she was insinuating that I didn't have any, but still, I laughed along with her, albeit a little sardonically.

"Will it be a witch wedding?" Gwyn asked. "For those are the best kinds. A proper shindig and some magickal potion?"

I picked up the parchment and scrutinised it for

the umpteenth time. "There's no mention of that, here."

"Lay it down," Gwyn urged. "Let me read it."

I placed it on the desk and she leaned over, quickly scanning the contents. Then she looked up and regarded me with surprise.

"Have you said yes to this?"

"Kind of." I'd emailed after Charity had left earlier, and said I needed to iron out a few issues and clarify details, but theoretically there shouldn't be a problem. I suppose I had in effect said yes. "Why?"

"Well I just wonder what you've let us all in for."

I fidgeted with the paperwork on my desk. I really needed to get on with some work. "How do you mean?"

"Sabien Laurent?" Gwyn pointed at the signature on the parchment with a long pale finger. "Aren't the Laurents a well-known vampire family?"

"Are they? No they're not. Are you sure?"

Gwyn nodded slowly.

"Oh no." I closed my eyes in dismay. What had I been thinking?

Gwyn tittered. "Vampires and witches, Alfhild? Now there's an explosive combination."

Grandmama was right of course, as she was about so many things.

A vampire? That explained the letter. The ancient parchment. It had probably been languishing in a drawer for hundreds of years. The elaborate handwriting. The red ink. Perhaps it wasn't ink at all. Perhaps it was blood.

My lip curled in distaste.

I'd never fully understood the enmity between witches and vampires, but I recognised a deep sense of unease within myself whenever I thought about them. Part of that was due to my upbringing. My mother, Yasmin, had always been deeply suspicious of them, and I'd long suspected this was simply an innate prejudice against a species so different from ours.

Any witch will tell you there are good witches and bad witches, white witches and black witches and every shade in between. I personally knew warlocks and mages, wizards and sages. But on the whole the witches I knew lived within a fluid and accepting creed. They worked with nature, harnessing natural forces, believing strongly in the tenet that what you send out into the universe will revisit you—tenfold.

My mother had claimed that vampires sucked

our energy. By their very parasitic nature, their urge to feed off humans whilst hiding in plain sight, tending to only show themselves under cover of the night, these things struck her as dastardly and ultimately cowardly. I could see why she had barely acknowledged the existence of those who moved within her social circle.

For my part, I'd met very few.

I slumped in my chair, wondering how to rescind my yes to the wedding event request. My thoughts were interrupted when the huge black Bakelite telephone on my desk rang, its throbbing vibration making the desk and all its contents, shake along with it.

I blinked in excitement, enjoying the sensation of butterflies flitting around my stomach. I had yet to become accustomed to people calling to make bookings, but now that I'd started to market the inn—both online and in specialist magazines and newspapers such as *The Celestine Times*—the phone was ringing more frequently with enquiries and potential bookings. I had to kerb my excitement every time I answered it. I'll be honest. I felt like a celebrity.

"Whittle Inn, good afternoon," I said, my voice as low and smooth as an Italian coffee (I thought anyway).

"Alfhild Daemonne?" The voice on the other end sounded equally as deep and rich. George Clooney with some sort of accent.

"Speaking."

"Ah, Alfhild. So good to reach you. It is Sabien Laurent here."

"Oh!" Quite coincidental that the very man I'd been thinking of had suddenly decided to call me. How prescient. I narrowed my eyes, suspecting telepathy or something dodgy and underhand.

"You sound surprised," Sabien said.

"I was just thinking about you. So yes, it is a surprise." I could place his accent now. French.

"How nice to be thought of. I hope it was all ze good things," he purred.

Yikes. Good things? Not really. How could I tell him my concerns?

I laughed nervously. "I was wondering whether Whittle Inn was the best location for your needs," I began. His accent brought out my very proper English one.

"It is perfection."

"You haven't seen it yet."

"I Googled it. It is in ze perfect location. How do you say, *magnifiquement rural*?"

"Rural," I repeated. "Yes. It is that."

"Nicely out of ze way."

Out of the way of what, I wondered. With any other client I know I would not have felt so suspicious, but my inner witch twitch was juddering like the rudder of a ship in a storm-tossed sea.

"We're just a small inn," I tried. "Without much in the way of fancy facilities."

"We will bring our own entertainment if that eez necessary."

The mind boggled. What would vampires consider entertainment? I imagined young virgins being forced to dance to some primitive drum beat in a clearing in Speckled Wood and shuddered. "That won't be necessary," I replied hastily. "We have a brilliant Elizabethan ensemble."

"*Splendide!*"

What was I doing? I seemed incapable of putting the man off. "But, but..." I cast around for another excuse. "Food. I mean... our chef... I'm not sure he can prepare the kind of delights you would find ... erm ... attractive."

"Do not worry, we are used to your British food. Your roast beef and Yorkshire puddings and your feesh and cheeps."

"Oh there'll be none of that," I said, properly aghast at the idea Whittle Inn would be serving up such mundane everyday culinary fare. "We have a proper chef. All the way from Paris." I gave a little shriek. I could have bitten off my own tongue.

"*C'est le meilleur résultat pour nous tous*, Alfhild?" he asked. "Surely this eez the best outcome for us all?"

I had to admit defeat.

"*Écoute*. The reason I was calling you today. I wondered if you would oblige me by visiting with my son in Hampstead, so that he can go through the finer details of his requirements with you. I know he would visit you himself but travelling can sometimes be a leetle bit challenging for our kind. I'm sure you comprehend zis."

"Well, I'm very busy at the moment, with the opening of the inn just over a week away."

"All expenses paid. First class. I will telegraph ze details and organise ze booking myself. *C'est une petite faveur, n'est-ce pas?*" When I didn't immediately answer he repeated, "It is a small favour, is it not?"

I closed my eyes in surrender.

Trust me to commit myself to a weird wedding on the very day my wonky inn re-opened.

CHAPTER SIX

Two days later, I arrived into Paddington Station in London. Exiting the railway station I found a rather swish limousine outside, the chauffeur clutching a clipboard with a version of my name— 'Demon'—scrawled across a familiar looking piece of parchment.

I made myself known to the driver and within seconds we were gliding away from the bustling station and moving easily through city traffic. I gazed out of the window, clocking those who turned to look as I floated past in my swanky automobile.

They think I'm famous, I thought to myself. Ha! Hardly.

The limousine pulled up outside a rather grand-looking block of private apartments. The 1930s façade, all stark clean lines and art deco windows, would have looked entirely at home on the set of an

Agatha Christie film set. The chauffeur unlocked an iron gate that led to the entrance of the building and showed me inside to the foyer.

"Take the lift up to the top floor," he said, the first words he had uttered since we'd met. He pressed the button for the elevator to check it was coming. "Mr Melchior Laurent is waiting for you there."

I nodded, resisting the urge to giggle at him, he seemed so austere. I watched him walk away until the ting of the bell alerted me to my ride and I stepped in. The back wall of the elevator had been covered with a floor-to-ceiling mirror, and given how harsh the lighting was, I could see every piece of fluff my clothes had accumulated on the journey thus far. I brushed myself down, tugging nervously at my long black skirt and fitted jacket, and tried to flatten my unruly hair. The elevator began to climb before I'd even pressed the button. Someone else had called it upstairs. It rose slowly, and I quickly cleaned a smudge of mascara from under my eye, checked my teeth were clean with a grimace and then smiled brightly at myself several times, as though practising a trick I'd never tried out before.

Arriving at the top floor—the penthouse suite I supposed—the elevator's bell announced me, and I stepped out onto the thick cream carpet of the vestibule. With only one other door in sight, there was no mistaking where I was heading next. My feet sunk into the floor and I glanced guiltily at my old black boots, hoping they were clean.

I waded across and tapped lightly on the door. It opened almost immediately, and I stared in surprise at an extremely tall and thin man with the most beautifully clear denim-blue eyes.

"Hi!" he said, without a trace of French accent. Not like his father at all. Perhaps he had lived here in London his whole life. "You must be Alfhild?" He reached out to shake my hand with just the right pressure. Neither too limp nor too firm. "Come in! Welcome to Laurent Towers."

I stepped into the hallway and he closed the door behind me. The walls in the hall were painted red, and the floor had dark wood. No carpet or rugs. I wondered whether the people living in the apartment below were troubled by the sound of people in the penthouse walking over the hard floor. And if they were, did they ever dare to complain?

There were no windows. A number of lamps cast mute lighting, but not enough to dispel the shadows.

"Call me Alf," I said automatically. This man wasn't what I'd been expecting at all. He was older than I'd assumed, maybe mid-thirties, with the beginnings of a receding hairline. What hair he had was blond, and cut short, but clumsily as though he had done his own barbering after a few beers. Pale and slender, at well over six feet, he towered above me by a good 8 or 9 inches.

"Alf," he repeated and smiled, his teeth white and even, and no obvious hint of fang. "I hope you had a pleasant journey?"

"It was uneventful and extremely comfortable in first class, thank you. I couldn't have asked for anything better."

He laughed. "May I offer you some refreshments? Marshmallows? Gin? Anything you like really. I'm sure I'll locate it somewhere."

I smiled, amused. *Marshmallows?* "I'd love some tea. I'm addicted to a good cup of tea."

"Coming right up." He nodded his head down the long hall and I followed him to the kitchen. "How do you take it?"

"A little milk, one sugar please." I couldn't believe my luck. Melchior came across as a perfect gentleman, nothing like the vampires my mother had warned me about.

"Is almond milk alright? Only I'm a vegetarian and Melchior doesn't drink milk."

I blinked in surprise. "You're not Melchior?"

Realising our mistake, he opened his eyes wide and pulled a face. "Oh no, sorry. I didn't introduce myself. How rude of me. I'm Marc. Marc Williams. I'm... well I'd like to say I'm one of Melchior's oldest friends, but given his advanced age, I'm probably a relatively new friend, as I've only been around for thirty or so years."

"Oh I see." I tried to hide my disappointment. Hopefully Melchior would be just as easy to get on with as Marc. Time would tell. Then my brain back-stepped through what he'd said. "Wait. You're a vegetarian?"

"Yes, I always have been." He waved the container of almond milk at me and I nodded for him to go ahead and add it to my mug.

"Doesn't that make being a vampire difficult?"

"Extremely." He grimaced. "I've adapted over the years, but even so, it's a blessing and a curse." He handed me my tea, so hot, the steam opened the pores on my face when I bent down to take a sip. "And you? You're a witch?"

"Not a particularly good one." I hurriedly blew on the scalding liquid to cool it down. "Hopefully getting better with time."

"That's all any of us can strive for," Marc responded with a gentle smile. "Let me take you through to see Melchior. He won't have been awake long, so do forgive him if he's a bit groggy."

I followed him along the hall. He paused and tapped at a door, listened for a moment and then pushed it open, walking into what can only be described as some kind of enormous mock-renaissance boudoir. I followed him in, gawping at the array of scantily clad stone statues arranged around a massive water feature in the centre of the over-heated room. The floor was marble, or mock-marble at least, and delicate silk curtains billowed as air was injected into the room through vents in the wall. The windows were tightly shuttered. Melchior was sprawled in a super-king-size bed, wearing little more than a black satin sheet.

He was not alone.

Two dark-haired beauties with milk-white skin had draped themselves around him and each other and were sound asleep, perfect rosebud mouths sighing in unison. They might have been sisters, twins even.

"Oh," I said, but the sound my mouth ejected sounded more like 'eww'.

"This is Alf," Marc said, oblivious to the odd scene playing out in front of us.

"Alf?" Melchior sat up and blinked at me, his eyes red and bleary.

"Alfhild Daemonne? Your father wants you to talk to her about the wedding, remember?"

"Oh drat. Yes." Like Marc, Melchior's accent was decidedly British.

Melchior nudged the two women lying either side of him. They opened their eyes, and one reached up to drag him back down next to her, but he clapped his hands irritably. "Go, go, go!"

I turned away to examine the water feature as the women slid out of bed and headed for the door. One of them came close and brushed past me, hissing as she did so. I recoiled in revulsion.

Yep. These were the vampires my mother had warned me about.

"I'll leave you two, to it, shall I?" Marc asked, and every bone and fibre in my being wanted to hold him back and yell, 'No, stay here and protect me', but of course I couldn't do that. Perhaps he could read my mind, for he winked at me conspiratorially. "If you need anything, I'll be down the hall in the kitchen preparing Melchior's breakfast."

I watched him go and turned back into the room with trepidation.

"Shall we get started?" Melchior asked, already

sounding bored. He indicated a seating area, next to the shuttered windows. The delicate curtains covered both blinds and shutters, and not a hint of the bright sunny afternoon infiltrated the room.

"Do you mind if I take my jacket off?" I asked. I was feeling the heat. Melchior shrugged and threw himself onto a chaise longue. Fortunately he was now wearing a long robe, which spared my blushes.

"Oh," he tutted and rubbed his eyes. "I should have asked Marc to being me a protein shake. I skipped dinner last night and I'm feeling the lack of iron a little today."

I shuddered. "Is Marc your friend or your manservant?" I asked curiously.

Melchior frowned in confusion. "Is there a difference?"

Taken aback, I thought about his response. Perhaps he was right. I certainly counted Florence and Zephaniah among my friends, and yet they worked for me. Some relationships can be complicated, can't they? I decided it would be better for me to plough on with discussing the organisation of the wedding. The sooner we hammered out the finer details the better. I fully intended to be back on the train to Devon before it began to get dark.

I pulled a clipboard and pen from my bag. "I need to clarify a few things with you."

"Well I can certainly tell you what I want which should make things easy for you." Melchior fixed me with his dark eyes. I was taken by the coldness in them, as though any sense of life had long been extinguished. The frigidity of his stare bled through my skin and sunk into my bones, and now I shivered despite the heat in the room.

"We can certainly try to—"

"There is no *try*, Alfhild. I take it you have never hosted a vampire wedding before?"

I held my tongue. Truth to tell, I'd never hosted a wedding full stop.

"I thought not."

The arrogance and rudeness of this young man was breath-taking.

"Sabien is paying for everything so you don't need to worry about the cost of anything." This much I knew, as Sabien had promised to deposit a sizeable amount of money in my bank account just as soon as I had met with Melchior. "He will supply the celebrant who will conduct our ceremony in the garden of the inn under the light of the Hunter's moon."

I blinked, curious about the reference. "I wasn't

aware that vampires were much bothered by phases of the moon?" Sabien had mentioned the importance of the moon ceremony too, but I was under the impression that such things were unimportant to vampires, in stark contrast to us witches, who used the moon cycle for all manner of magickal rites and spell workings.

"Some old hag somewhere has brainwashed Sabien into thinking that marrying at midnight on the 31st October under the Hunter's moon will guarantee him, me, and any of my offspring, a long and auspicious immortality with great prosperity." Melchior picked at his ear. "For some reason those things are important to him."

"But not to you?"

"I couldn't care less whether I was married in a witch's hovel in the countryside... or a *hay loft*, quite frankly." His eyes bore into mine and I shifted uncomfortably, bristling at his slur on my inn. The reference to The Hay Loft was deliberate. He'd been checking me out.

"*Cessabit*," I hissed under my breath, calming the indignant fizz of my rising blood pressure and imagining water from a deep-rooted natural spring running through my veins and over my skin, cleansing me and soothing my ire.

When I had control I met his dead stare again and smiled, lifting my pen to begin writing. "So you'll supply the celebrant," I agreed, keeping my tone light and gracious. Something in his gaze shifted, like oil on water, slippery and dark. He didn't like the fact that I'd regained control of myself.

"I'd like you to organise the flowers. Twelve dozen wild-grown red roses, and similar in black, complete with thorns, to decorate a ceremonial arch, fixed to a raised dais in the garden. I assume you have workmen who can create such a thing." His tone was clipped and business-like now, the sardonic drawl, previously evident, had disappeared.

"A buffet, heavy on the raw meat, perhaps some exotic subtleties. My understanding is you have a French chef in situ. He can create a good spread for our *mortal* guests." Melchior sneered.

I wrote everything down as he looked on.

"I'm sure you can attend to the finer details. Wedding stuff. Make it look good." He waved his hands, dismissing me.

"When will you arrive?" I asked.

"Overnight on the 28th. You'll need to arrange for our rooms to be completely blacked out." I made a note of that. This would keep Zephaniah busy. We didn't really have a great deal of time. We needed to get on with it.

"What is the size of your party?" I asked.

Melchior suppressed a yawn. "Oh the dull mundanity of all this organisation," he said. "Let's say twenty. Can your grim rural hovel cope do you think?"

Just about. At maximum capacity the inn could hold forty, but that meant shared bedrooms.

"You haven't mentioned the bride," I said, ignoring his jibe.

"Should I?" he asked in surprise. "How dull. Anyone would think this was all about her."

This was probably the single most shocking thing he'd come out with so far. I looked up from my clipboard and regarded him in consternation. "I suppose most weddings generally are very bride-oriented."

"Boring, boring, boring!"

I glared at him. "What's her name? Can I start with that?"

"Ekaterina Lukova."

"Is she bringing family and guests too?"

"Oh this is tedious," Melchior cried.

I took a deep breath. "Did you include her party in your numbers?"

"Yes, yes!"

"Great," I said and picked up my bag to stuff the clipboard and pen away.

Melchior rolled around on the chaise longue so that he was on his front. He watched me, his eyes narrow. "One thing," he said.

"Yes?" I paused.

"We will supply a headdress, a very important piece of ceremonial ware. When it is delivered you must take very good care of it."

"No problem. I'll make sure of that myself."

"We'll also supply her dress, and one of my guests will be her bridesmaid and attend to hair and make-up etc. We will not require the services of anyone else."

"Very well." I stood and zipped my bag, then pulled my jacket on. I couldn't wait to get out in the fresh air. When I turned back to him to bid goodbye and shake his hand he was standing mere inches away from me, staring down into my face. I hadn't heard or seen him approach. He'd moved like lightning, without so much as disturbing the air.

I gasped, and he leaned down even closer, his face centimetres from mine. I wriggled away, my calf muscles rubbing against the seat behind me, trapping me from escape.

"You're a beautiful woman, for a witch, Alfhild."

He plucked a lock of my long curly hair, twirling it between his fingers. "Where are you staying tonight? Perhaps I can pay you a visit? We could share dinner." He drew a finger down the side of my neck, an intimate gesture I simply couldn't stand for.

I yanked my head sideways, freeing my hair, and with a supreme effort of will side-stepped. He lay a hand on my shoulder and laughed into my face. I shrank from his breath and the stench of a thousand years of dismal culinary choices.

"*Scintillam!*" I said clearly. Yellow sparks erupted from my shoulders like sparklers at a child's party and just as quickly disappeared. He jerked his hand away in pain.

He howled and sucked on his fingers. "What was that?"

"*That* was a little lesson, Melchior Laurent. A short sharp shock. And believe me, there will be more where that came from. Allow us at Whittle Inn the pleasure of hosting your wedding, by all means, but if you're coming down to Whittlecombe, you will treat me, and my staff and all of the guests at the inn with the utmost respect. What is it the Christian peoples say? Do unto others as you would have them do unto you? Let this be your warning. The inn, my staff, and the villagers of Whittlecombe are entirely off limits to you and any of your kind. No hunting. No maiming. No killing. Is that clear?"

Melchior dropped his hands to his side and beamed at me.

"Oh you are wonderful!" He grinned. "*A femme de feu*, as my father would say. I'm so looking forward to spending more time with you."

"I'll see you on the twenty-eighth," I responded sharply, and he threw his head back, laughing like a drain.

Marc saw me out. We stood together by the elevator, watching as the little gold arrow slowly ran in a semi-circle to indicate each floor it passed as it climbed towards us.

"Tough crowd, huh?" he asked, observing my straight back and uninviting expression no doubt.

"You could say that." I exhaled and dropped my shoulders.

"I'm sure you'll do a sterling job."

"I hope so. That's my intention at any rate." I relaxed a little more. "May I ask you a question?"

"Of course. Anything."

"Regarding the need for blood…" I paused

wondering if this was a delicate conversation. "I want to make sure everyone at the inn is safe, you know, for the duration."

"Oh yes, don't worry about that. We're all mod-cons these days. The Laurents have a portable blood bank."

"A blood bank?" I twisted my face up. "That's grim. No offence."

"None taken. It's not ideal, but it's a useful temporary solution. They'll set it up outside, and it can be used with complete discretion."

I shook my head. You learn something new every day. "I'm not surprised the other hotel passed up the opportunity to host the Laurent nuptials."

"Other hotel?" Marc asked, frowning. "There was no other hotel. I'm pretty sure it was supposed to be Whittle Inn all along."

Chapter Seven

Wherever you may wander, there is no place like home.

As I stumbled into Whittle Inn shortly before midnight, the stresses and strains of the day oozed out of my body. The faint scent of freshly baked bread, and for some strange reason, oranges, permeated throughout the downstairs of the inn. Someone had thoughtfully left a light on in the bar, so I dumped my belongings in the porch and made my way through, running a weary hand over my face. Travelling first class is unbeatable, but you don't actually get anywhere any faster than anyone travelling in a lower class. There's just slightly more leg room and people pretend to be nice to you. I'd spent the best part of twelve hours on the road and I was exhausted.

I considered pouring myself a night-cap—the

display of drinks behind the bar looked appetising—but the faint sound of voices from beyond the frosted glass door stopped me in my tracks. Thoughts of Melchior had followed me all the way home, and while I couldn't imagine he would trail me and harm me tonight, that hadn't stopped me worrying.

I opened the door and crept through the back hallway. The Nook and the Snug were closed up and dark, the voices coming from the kitchen. I paused at the foot of the stairs. Whomever was conversing sounded cheerful enough. I poked my head around the door.

Florence and Charity.

"Hey!" I said, surprised to see them there together.

"Good evening, Miss Alf," Florence smiled. "Welcome home."

"It is so good to be back." I groaned and plopped myself down on a kitchen bench opposite Charity.

"I thought you'd only been gone today?" Charity looked puzzled.

"Let me tell you, it has been the longest day of my life." I kicked my boots off under the table and wiggled my toes. Somewhere my mother was spinning in her grave.

"Florence said you had a meeting in London."

"Mm," I said, glancing around to see if Florence was planning on dishing up some supper. As usual, she didn't let me down. I watched her cut up a gala pie and lay a slice on a plate. The kettle boiled away on the stove. Tea wouldn't be long. "I met with a vampire named Melchior Laurent. He's the groom of the wedding you talked me into hosting."

"I talked you into?" Charity repeated with a smile.

"You did. I was ready to say no," I declared, and then winked at her.

Charity sat up straight and gaped at me. "Wait. Wait. What? You said... vampire."

"Yes." I shook my head, only now realising how big a mistake I'd made. "That was a small detail I hadn't really paid attention to, until Grandmama pointed it out. So I went to meet the younger Mr Laurent today, and he turned out to be my worst nightmare."

Charity shook her head. "I don't know whether to take you seriously."

I indicated Florence, smouldering away by the stove as she poured water into the pot. "You're sitting at a kitchen table with a witch, being served tea by a woman who's been dead for over a century, but is still burning, and you're not sure whether I'm telling the truth?"

"You have a point," Charity said, and we laughed together. Florence observed us with a wry shake of her head.

"Why are you here at this time, anyway?"

"I've been working the late shift at The Hay Loft. It wasn't a great few hours. I'll spare you the details. Anyway, I quit. With immediate effect. I came up here to let you know. And to say, that if you'll have me, I can start here any time you like."

"Really?" I asked, squeaking with excitement. "That's great news."

"Oh good!" Charity clapped her hands. "I was hoping you'd say that."

I took a mouthful of pie and chewed hard. "You know, there's a room on the top floor you're welcome to have. I know you and your Mum don't live that far away, but if you wanted your own space it would be perfect. I set it aside for the new chef, but seeing as Monsieur Emietter is a spirit, he doesn't need a bedroom. Funny how things work out."

"That does sound perfect." Charity nodded.

"If the weather turns bad this winter you'll be glad of it."

"Nah, it never snows in Devon," Charity said

with total conviction. "Something to do with the Gulf stream."

"Oh well, that's good," I replied. "I don't like snow anyway."

The following afternoon Charity arrived at the inn carrying some of her belongings in two huge holdalls. I hardly recognised her.

She had visited the hairdresser and hadn't held back.

The long hair had gone, replaced by a much shorter style in a bright flamingo pink.

"Wow," I said.

"I know," Charity dropped her bags and spun around, treating me to a 360-degree view of her new style. "Do you like it?"

"I love it!" I pointed to my own red head. "I think we may clash though."

Charity smirked, "It will be fine if we're never seen in public together."

I showed her to her room, and then took her up into the attic and introduced her to the ghosts who resided there, explaining to them that Charity was my manager and second-in-command. I shot Gwyn a look when I said this, but she didn't seem unduly perturbed, and although she kept darting glances at Charity's new hairdo every minute or so, she seemed to have taken a liking to her quicker than I had hoped for.

For her part Charity was entranced both by the ghosts, and by the piles of junk in the attic. She poked around among chests and pulled the dust sheets off the large portraits and pieces of furniture stored under the eaves, clucking and tutting whenever she found something of note.

I finally managed to drag her away and called a meeting in the bar to talk everyone through our plans for the wedding and the opening of the inn. Monsieur Emietter was in attendance with Gwyn translating for me, along with Zephaniah, Luppitt Smeatharpe and the leader of the Devonshire Fellows, Robert Wait, and Florence of course.

"Whittle Inn is going to be hosting what is ostensibly the vampire wedding of the century," I announced." I have my doubts about this but I'm going to keep them to myself for now. What I need is for us to pull together and make this an event that people will talk about for years to come. We need to put Whittle Inn back on the map."

I glanced over at Charity who was taking notes.

"I didn't get masses of detail from Melchior Laurent yesterday, but he has a party of around twenty. For the wedding itself, it will take place at midnight on Halloween, and he wants a raised dais area with a rose arbour. Oh, and that needs to be outside."

"He wants the wedding outside? At night? That late in October? What's the forecast?" Charity asked.

"That's your first job." I smiled.

Charity whistled and made a note.

"Can you also take charge of the arbour?" I asked. "Mr Laurent Senior sent me a list of suppliers for flowers. They've asked for red and black roses."

"Well of course they have. Not exactly thinking out of the box, these vampires are they?" Charity said, and I do believe my great grandmother snorted in amusement.

I continued. "Zephaniah? Not all of these guests will be vampires by the sound of it, but we need to make sure the bedrooms that the vampires do have access to, are all fitted with blackout blinds." I reiterated this. "That's vitally important. The slightest hint of daylight and that will be the end of the bride and groom and family." Zephaniah doffed an imaginary hat.

"Oh and can you take charge of the dais and arbour thingie please? Ned can help you. And my father if he's around." I hadn't seen Erik for a few weeks, so I assumed he was off somewhere doing his Circle of Querkus duty.

"Grandmama?" I turned to Gwyn and Monsieur Emietter. The vampires don't necessarily need food, but they will have non-vampire guests, and we will have people up from the village, so I want a decent spread." I checked my notes. "And Melchior Laurent asked for raw meat."

I stuck my tongue out in a disgusted motion and Gwyn eyed me with disdain. "Really, Alfhild. The French love rare meat. Not all food has to be charred in a bonfire, you know."

"What about a cake?" asked Florence.

I ran a quick eye down my notes. "They never mentioned a cake to me."

"Every wedding has a cake," said Charity. She had a fair point.

"Ooh, Miss Alf. Please let me make the cake, if Monsieur Emietter doesn't mind of course." Florence dipped a curtsey at the chef and he stared at her, not comprehending what she was saying. I had to organise some English lessons for the man, or the rest of us would have to learn French. One of the two.

"If Monsieur Emietter doesn't mind, you can make the cake, Florence." I nodded in agreement and

Florence clasped her hands together and squealed in delight.

"Better make it a red and black one," Charity muttered, her gaze focused on her list.

"That's probably not a bad idea," I said. "Let's pander to the stereotype. Multi-tiered. Gothic looking."

"A spider web or two," Charity continued. "It is Halloween after all."

Florence glanced uncertainly between me and Charity. "Charity is joking," I said. Although I wasn't entirely sure she was. "Go with whatever you think best."

"I'll make the most wonderful cake any bride has ever seen." Florence's eyes shone.

The phone behind the bar rang, and Charity, who was closest, picked it up.

"Whittle Inn, good afternoon. Charity speaking, how may I help you?" she sang, and I hid a smile.

"Hello. Yes? I'm the new manager. Yes. Yes, she is. Okay. One second." She held the phone out to me. "DS Gilchrist. He says it's important."

CHAPTER EIGHT

The following morning, just after eight, I was standing outside Whittle Allotments with a huge bunch of keys, waiting for George to arrive. It was a cool morning, with the promise of more sunshine, and a fine lingering mist was already beginning to burn off on the hills surrounding Whittlecombe. I absently watched as tendrils of steamy dew evaporated into the warm air, until George drew up in his battered silver Volvo and joined me outside the big iron gates.

Whittle Allotments had been in existence since the First World War when many villagers were struggling on their rations. Every family who inhabited a house belonging to the Whittle Estate had been 'allotted' a piece of ground on which to grow vegetables to help sustain them through shortages. Over the years they had continued to prove popular, and during the Great Depression of the 1930s, the Second World War, and the period of austerity that followed, the allotments had proved their value time and time again. Nowadays, not every cottage made use of their allotments, because in the early twenty-first century, the ready availability of food meant busy families had plenty of alternatives. I could see that some of the allotments lay unkempt and uncared for, and I made a mental note to check on ways to hire the land out to those who wanted it locally, or perhaps increase plot sizes for those who worked their patches.

"Morning!" I greeted George. He darted a quick glance all around to check for anyone watching us, then gave me a quick hug.

"How are you doing?" he asked.

"I'm fine. But you look tired."

"Oh I'm juggling several cases at once. I didn't get to bed till gone two this morning."

"I'll treat you to coffee afterwards if you like. Keep you going throughout today." I jangled the keys. "What are you expecting to find here anyway?"

"I don't know," George said as we walked the few steps to the entrance. "Derek Pearce's neighbours said he spent most days down here, from dawn till dusk apparently. Until a few weeks ago at any rate, when he stopped going out altogether, apart from a few walks with the dog. I spoke to Stan and Rhona in the General Stores, and they couldn't recall seeing him either."

"He became reclusive?"

"That's what his neighbours are saying."

"Oh that's a shame." My stomach dropped. He had been one of my tenants. Was there anything I could have done? Visited him? Offered him assistance in some way?

"He wasn't an old man," George continued, verbalising his thoughts. "I can't help wondering whether he felt threatened in some way?"

By The Mori no doubt. I didn't want to utter their name aloud, so I kept quiet.

I tried the gate and was surprised to find it already unlocked, but the reason became clear as soon as we stepped through. Three or four villagers, older gentlemen in the main, were already hard at work, each on their allotted patch of ground, weeding, pruning, picking, and in once case burning a pile of rubbish. The air was sweetly scented with his bonfire.

"Early risers," George mumbled, observing them with mock disgust. "They must be mad. When I retire I don't intend to drag myself out of bed much before mid-morning." When the old-timers looked our way curiously, Gilchrist waved cheerily and made his way over to the closest gentleman.

"Good morning, sir. DS Gilchrist." George took out his warrant card and opened it.

The old chap looked at it and him. "Bob Gretchen." He looked my way and nodded curtly. "That's the maid from up at the inn?"

"Alfhild Daemonne, yes."

"Come to check out the allotments has she? I've heard she's intending to sell them off." He spoke to George and didn't address me even though I was less than twenty feet away. I stared at him, my forehead creased in indignation at his unnecessary hostility.

George shot me a look that seemed to suggest I should back off.

"I'm not aware that's the case," George replied smoothly as I moved away in the opposite direction, "but you should take that up with Ms Daemonne. She seems a sensible woman really."

I tittered quietly. I'd have to relieve poor George of that notion soon.

While George finished asking his questions I counter-navigated the edge of the allotments, underneath some towering pine trees to my right along the rough stone-strewn path there, walking extra slowly to allow him more time to catch me up.

When he did so, he smirked at me. "Old Bob there is not your greatest fan. What have you done to upset him?"

I shook my head. "I really don't know. I don't even recall coming across him before."

"He lives with his daughter, let me see," George checked his notebook, "Grace Gretchen in Dandelion Cottage."

"Dandelion? Oh I know it. Come to think of it, I remember his daughter too." I grimaced. Dandelion was one of my cottages most in need of TLC. Painted white, once upon a time, it was now grey and weathered. I'd had some emergency repairs done to the cottage over the summer, in particular the guttering which must have been fifty years old, but hadn't found the tenants overly helpful when it came to allowing tradesmen on their property to conduct repairs. In fact, if I remembered correctly, Grace Gretchen was a sour-faced shrew.

However, I didn't tell George that. Sometimes the things we say and the things we think reflect badly on ourselves when we release them to the ether. Far better to be mindful and generous, I decided. Perhaps Grace had been having a bad day when I'd met her previously. Perhaps I had been over-officious or seemed judgemental. Life is a constant striving for balance after all.

George looked at me sideways, and grinned. "My what a busy mind you have."

I thumped his arm. "Where are we headed now?"

Pointing to a shed to the rear of the allotments, he picked up the pace and I scurried after him. "It's this one," he said as we halted in front of the ramshackle structure. Yes it had once been a shed, and painted green to blend with its surroundings, but numerous parts had been added on with corrugated iron and planks of wood, and now the paint was flaking off and the iron had rusted. The roof had been felted numerous times, and thick sheets of plastic and canvas were tacked on here and there to ensure everything remained weather-tight.

"Crikey," I said and surveyed the rest of the plot this astounding piece of architecture inhabited. It wasn't much better. Any vegetables that had grown here had been gifted to foragers of the small mammalian or insect varieties. In one corner of the plot, the vines from beans had run amok and taken over everything in close vicinity, like some weird be-tentacled parasite. Elsewhere brambles were over-running the fruit plots, and potatoes were rotting in a maggot infested pile.

Perplexed I pointed at the beans. "You know, I'm not big on gardening, but these must have been planted earlier this year. Left to their own devices, surely they would have died back over the winter?"

George nodded. "Derek intended to take care of this plot as recently as a few months ago, so why did he stop?"

"In any case, I thought you said he was here from dawn till dusk," I ventured as we gingerly picked our way through the vegetation, to the door of the shed.

"According to the neighbours."

"It doesn't look like he's been here in months," I said.

"Bob says he used to be here day in and day out until a few weeks ago, but recently he'd abandoned his plants and remained in the shed. Bob would see smoke coming from the chimney."

"Odd." I fished the bunch of keys out again and looked for the most likely ones to fit the lock. None of them looked likely. I half-heartedly tried a few.

"Let me have a look." George examined first the keys and then the lock. "Stand back," he said and put his shoulder to the door. With one almighty heave, the door flew open easily.

George stepped through and I followed.

I had imagined that the inside of the shed would look like every other shed I'd ever seen, full of gardening implements, ladders, chairs and old paint cans. Derek Pearce's shed was nothing like that. It kind of resembled a small front room. There was one easy chair, faded with age but relatively clean, a wood burning stove with a chimney that opened through the roof, a two-ring stove with a whistling camping kettle and a saucepan atop of it, and small cupboards covered by gingham checked curtains, hung on wire, rather than solid doors. There were several worn rugs on the floor and a comfortable looking dog basket close to the fire. Next to the chair some books and numerous newspapers were piled up on a small occasional table.

"He wasn't living here," I said. "There's no bed, but otherwise it's certainly comfortable enough."

George pointed to a few framed photos hanging on the wall. One of a young woman with a Golden Labrador taken many years ago judging by the sepia tones of the print, and one of an older woman smiling into the camera that looked more recent. "His wife."

"Oh," I breathed. "He missed her." My forehead felt tight and tears pricked at my eyes, sad for Derek.

George glanced at me. "You old silly," he said and gave me a quick hug.

"I know. I can't help it. I hate it when people are unhappy." I smiled, my eyes watery. "It really affects me. It's an empathic trait many witches have. I wish I could have done more for him."

"You couldn't have done anything, you didn't know him."

"Didn't he have any family at all?" I asked.

"None that we've been able to trace so far. Derek, and Sarah—his wife—had a son, but the lad was killed in a motorcycling accident in the mid-nineties. Sarah died five years ago."

"So tragic." I was beginning to feel worse.

"We haven't been able to locate any siblings for Derek. Sarah has an older sister, but she's been living in Australia for over forty years."

"You'll have to give me the contact details. I'll need to make arrangements for disposal of the belongings."

"I've been in contact with her already, so I'll mention that to her," George said.

I parted the curtains of one of the cupboards. Cannisters containing teabags, coffee, Hob-Knobs and dog biscuits on one shelf, two mugs, a couple of plates and bowls on the shelf below, and tins of soup on the bottom shelf.

George was flicking through the newspapers on the table. "This paper is recent, just eight days ago," he remarked and held it up, so I could see it. The crossword had been partially completed.

"Derek had been coming here but not doing any work on his plot. I wonder why."

"Perhaps he had been ill. We should get the pathologist's report later today. I'll check his medical records with the Whittlecombe Health Centre too."

I pulled the curtain back on another cupboard, a taller one this time, unleashing an acrid smell. "Phew, what's that?" I asked and staggered back, blinking.

George pulled me away and hand over his mouth and nose peered more closely. "What a stink," he said. Taking a pen from his pocket he poked at something on a shelf. "Okay I think we need to get out of here."

"What is it?" I asked, my voice raised in alarm. "What's wrong? What did you see?"

"White crystals. I think Derek has been storing some sort of chemicals here. I need to get some forensic specialists in here to take a closer look."

I tried to peer over his shoulder, but George

grabbed me and pushed me out of the shed. "Health and safety and all that," he said, his eyebrows knitted with concern. "Out you go."

"You're a spoilsport!" I pouted.

"Listen I'm a police officer and responsible for public safety. Besides you know I'd hate it if anything happened to you." He leaned forward to kiss my forehead before firmly closing the door. Having burst it in he couldn't now secure it properly.

Pausing outside on the overgrown patch of land, I listened to George call the situation in to the police station. I touched the part of my forehead where his lips had been, feeling an energy pulse there, then dissipate outwards, making me tingle from head to toe.

CHAPTER NINE

The 27th October dawned bright and sunny. Leaves clung to the trees, reluctant to let go of the marvellous summer we had enjoyed. The kaleidoscope of autumnal colours dancing in dappled sunlight filled my soul with joy as I enjoyed an early-morning walk in the garden of Whittle Inn. Sadly, my contemplative reverie was soon disturbed by the sound of sawing and hammering.

Zephaniah and Ned had set to with gusto and now the raised dais, measuring approximately 15 feet square, along with the arched arbour, were beginning to take shape. I stood and admired their handiwork for some time, but then left them to it and headed indoors for some peace and quiet.

Theoretically.

The inn was coming alive. Deliveries of food and drink were arriving on an hourly basis. Food went straight to the back door while the alcohol either came in the front or was taken around to the drop at the side of the inn, leading to the cellar. Charity had overseen the installation of new pump equipment and at last Whittle Inn had real ale and a local sparkling cider on tap. Florence took pride in making the brasses gleam on the pumps, while I was itching to start pulling pints.

Charity was currently 'dressing' the inn. This seemed to involve the Wonky Inn Clean-up Crew moving various items from the attic to bedrooms and public rooms. A variety of lamps for example had been cleaned, painted and re-homed, topped with brand new brightly-coloured silk lampshades.

Antique jug and bowl sets had been washed and dried, and placed on dressing tables in guest bedrooms—purely for effect Charity told me—and books had been brought down, dusted and arranged on shelves.

Now I watched as a dozen large portraits and paintings were carefully moved down the stairs, ready for hanging. Chief among these was the portrait of Alfhild Gwynfyre Daemonne. Her ghost followed it on its journey, clucking whenever it made contact with a wall or stair banister.

"Where are you hanging that?" I asked Charity,

the trepidation in my voice obvious. Gwyn glared at me.

"In the bar," Charity replied, and raised her eyebrows to offer me a brook-no-arguments look.

"In the bar?" I repeated. "No offence Grandmama but I'm not sure our guests will want to look at you while they're enjoying a drink. It will put them off."

Charity folded her arms, and Gwyn mimicked her. They stood side by side, heads identically cocked, glowering at me.

"I happen to think it's a wonderful painting," Charity told me. "The best of the bunch. It deserves to take pride of place here in the hub of the inn. It's had a good clean and it's in remarkable condition. Trust me, with the right lighting your Grandmama is going to glow and illuminate the whole room. People from far and wide will admire it."

Next to Charity, Gwyn preened openly. I wasn't sure whether to laugh or cry at the idea of anyone admiring my crotchety great grandmother, so I scowled back at them. "Well, you seem to know what you're doing."

"Of course she does," Gwyn interjected. "Charity is the best decision *you've* made since you turned up in Whittlecombe."

"Thanks," I said.

"Oh one of them surely?" said Charity and giggled. "I thought promoting Florence to head housekeeper was an inspired decision."

"What are you talking about?" I asked. *Had I lost a day somewhere?* "I haven't promoted Florence."

"You haven't? Oh that must have been me as well then."

"You promoted Florence?"

"I did."

"Charity—" I began and then stopped. Thinking it about it, that *did* seem like an inspired decision. It was just a pity it hadn't been mine.

"Not to mention hiring Monsieur Emietter," Gwyn chimed in.

I pulled a face. Gwyn was right about that too. His food was amazing. I'd already put on a kilo and my skirts were feeling tight. Given my general tendency to curviness, it was something I would have to keep an eye on.

I sniffed. "Okay, okay. I can see I'm surplus to requirements."

Charity laughed. "Gwyn, we have to stop. We're hurting Alf's feelings." Gwyn smirked and turned to oversee proceedings as her portrait was lifted into pride of place above the large fireplace in the bar.

Charity wrapped her arm around my shoulders. "I'm only kidding, honestly."

"I know," I said and hugged her back. Truth to tell, *she* was the best decision I had made. Charity was helping me make my dream become a reality. I might have achieved it without her, but she added imagination and pizzazz and a healthy dose of fun.

Standing back I tilted my head this way and that. Charity was right. The portrait did appear to glow. Whether it was a trick of the light, or due to the paint used, I couldn't say. Grandmama gazed out at the bar from between the edges of the gilt frame, surveying the world with imperious majesty. The angle of her chin, the glint in her eye and the slight curve of her lips told the viewer that everything was right with her world, and therefore by extension, right with theirs.

After lunch I headed down into the village to pay another visit to Derek's cottage. Sarah Pearce's older sister had instructed me to pass her sister and brother-in-law's valuables on to a solicitor in Exeter, so she could arrange valuation and have them auctioned. Everything else was to be offered to charity or given away.

I'd been visiting the sad little cottage for a few hours a day and working my way through each room, boxing, bagging and binning. Considering Sarah and Derek had lived in this cottage since they'd been married in 1976, their belongings were scant. I had the sense that Derek may have already worked his way through the house in the years since Sarah had died, ridding himself of all her possessions and the memories that went with them.

That's not to say that he hadn't cherished her. I really believe he had. I found small mementos— photos of her hidden away in his bedside drawer, in the pages of a book he'd been reading, and a threadbare and well-loved teddy bear on her bedside table, along with one of her jumpers, tucked under the pillows on her side too.

I hadn't lingered long in the main bedroom. The police had boarded up the window in there and it was darker than the rest of the house. Memories of the spinning orb unnerved me and had me glancing over my shoulder or starting at the slightest noise.

It was with relief that I moved on to the rest of the house. The spare bedroom was virtually empty. Once upon a time this would have been their son's room. The only nod to his existence were the naked single bed, a poster on the wall of Marilyn Manson, and a pile of CDs on a shelf in the corner. The wardrobes and cupboards were devoid of contents. I rattled around the room, filling up my cardboard box with the CDs and a random beermat, yanking open drawers and cupboards and quickly closing them again when all they contained was stale air and the memory of belongings.

Nothing to see.

Or so I thought.

Pulling open the bottom drawer of the son's chest of drawers, I automatically began to close it again when I spotted a pale manila folder tucked into the corner. Coloured beige, it was well-camouflaged and would have been easy to overlook.

Assuming it was school work I tossed it into my box, but the sheath of paper contained within scattered and I realised they were actually bank statements. I picked up the box and rescued the paper, arranging them on top of the chest of drawers to take a closer look.

It felt wrong, looking back at someone's personal finances, but I couldn't stop myself. I flicked through the pages, each one a month's statement from the same national bank, dating back for the past five years or so. There were relatively few transactions. Monthly payments to Whittle Estates for rent and the hire of the allotment, direct debits for gas, electricity, council tax, TV license, phone, and water. Every Monday, £50 cash was drawn from the post office here in Whittlecombe. Derek didn't have a car.

That was it.

One man's lonely routine.

I was about to put the statements back into the file to pass onto George when one payment caught my eye.

£30,000.

A serious amount of money for a man like Derek.

The money had been deposited in his account from a company named Astutus Holdings. I rifled through the rest of the statements but couldn't find a deposit of that amount anywhere else, and no further deposits from that company. This was a one off. Possibly Derek had inherited money or sold something valuable. Maybe he'd had shares.

Perhaps it was none of my business.

Nonetheless I pulled my mobile from my bag and took a few photos of the statements, then I bundled the folder up to pass onto the police.

There might not have been anything out of the ordinary in this single financial transaction, but I couldn't shake the feeling that Derek had been in deep with The Mori. I intended to send the photos to Wizard Shadowmender. He would have contacts who would be able to dip a little deeper into Astutus. Penelope Quigwell would probably be one of those.

Pocketing my mobile, I closed the door of the bedroom. That was the upstairs of Primrose Cottage packed up. Time to tackle downstairs.

It had been a long and trying day, and by the time I returned home to Whittle Inn a fiery sun was setting behind the hills, and the sky was painted in plum and pastel pinks. I'd been looking forward to a decent dinner, but Monsieur Emietter barred me from the kitchen as he was far too busy preparing mock-ups of the wedding feast.

I had to settle for a cheese and tomato sandwich and a packet of crisps, supplied by Florence, who hopped anxiously around me while I ate it at my desk in the office, dusting things that didn't need dusting and knocking my papers to the floor every time she floated past. Eventually I asked her to stop.

"Are you alright, Florence? You seem a little nervy."

"Nervy? No miss."

"Okay." I returned my attention to my laptop, busily uploading the photos from my phone, while composing a letter to Wizard Shadowmender. Two minutes later a potted plant flew off the window sill, and Mr Hoo, who had been dozing there, shot into the room in alarm, soaring past me into the bedroom where he perched on the bedframe and twitted consolingly to himself.

"Florence? Is there a reason you're trying to frighten my poor owl to death?"

"No, no, miss. Sorry, miss."

I scanned her face for clues and decided she *did* want to speak to me. I rocked back on my chair and picked up my packet of crisps. "What's up?" I asked and began to munch. Boy, I was famished.

"About what Miss Charity said earlier today, Miss Alf."

I stared at Florence blankly.

"About me being housekeeper, miss."

"Oh that!"

Florence hesitated. "You... I... well..."

"What?" I took one more large mouthful and twisted the plastic packet expertly into a little triangle. Florence carefully watched me and then lifted her head.

"I couldn't presume, based on what Miss Charity said, that... well... you know? I know she's the manager now, but... well you're still the person in charge, Miss Alf."

"Oh, I see." I was touched. "You're asking whether your new appointment is official?"

"Yes, miss."

I grinned. "Oh of course, Florence! It's a wonderful idea. I'd give you a pay rise but seeing as I don't pay you anyway, you'll just have to settle for an imaginary one."

Florence laughed, and I joined in, pleased with her delight. "Try not to let it go to your head," I said, my face deadly serious, but when I winked at her she emitted another peel of laughter.

"Oh I won't, I promise! Thank you, Miss Alf."

She began to apparate and I quickly stopped her. "Just one thing?"

"Yes, miss?" She was so translucent I could see the fireplace behind her. She reminded me of the Cheshire Cat in *Alice's Adventures in Wonderland.*

"Sneak into the kitchen and find me some cake, can you, please? I'm going to fade away to nothing if I don't have something else to eat."

"I doubt that, miss." Florence giggled saucily, and looked at me pointedly. Then she was gone before I could change my mind about her new appointment.

I finished off an unhealthily large slice of Victoria Sponge with clotted cream and home-made raspberry jam a little later while languishing in the bath. The scent of lavender soothed me, and I lay back staring through the open window, watching the steam escape. Mr Hoo perched in his customary position half-in and half-out, his head turning this way and that, laser beam eyes searching the grounds below for his own supper. From somewhere in the distance I could hear the muffled sounds of a drum and some kind of squawking instrument. An Elizabethan dance. No doubt Luppitt Smeatharpe and the Devonshire Fellows were rehearsing for the wedding.

Tonight the rhythm soothed rather than irritated, and I relaxed into the warm water, lulled into a false sense of security, closing my eyes and drifting away.

Half-asleep, the beating of the drums began to get louder, as though they were moving closer, and closer still, until instead of drums, I imagined I could hear the pounding hooves of dozens of heavy horses.

"Alf!" Charity's cry ripped through the inn and I shot upright in the bath, sending a cascade of water sloshing over the sides. Mr Hoo, having had enough scares for one night, took to wing and soared out of sight in the direction of the nearest cluster of trees. "Alf?"

"What is it?" I shouted, scrambling out of the bath and slipping around in the water on the floor. I grabbed my towel. The sound of hooves over gravel was unmistakeable.

"We've got company," Charity screeched back. "They've arrived early!"

I skidded to the window, holding my towel against my front to preserve my modesty, and leaned over the sill. The night was dark, and Whittlecombe village gave out little in the way of light pollution. Squinting, my heart thumping hard in my chest, I could just about make out some illuminations bobbing in the distance, moving down the lane at quite a pace. As the shapes drew closer I could see these illuminations were old-fashioned gas lights, glowing blue.

I stared in amazement. Coming up the drive, scattering shards of gravel left, right and centre, and slowing to a trot in front of the inn, were six blinkered black horses, with tall plumes of shiny black feathers standing above their forelocks. The team of horses were pulling a black hearse carriage, its blinds drawn so that no-one could see within.

Behind this first one, came another. And another. In fact there must have been a dozen carriages and a dozen hearses, each drawn by six beautiful black horses and each containing a coffin.

The vampires had arrived at Whittle Inn.

Chapter Ten

Twenty-four hours ahead of schedule, Whittle Inn received its first guests.

Trembling in anticipation, I rapidly dried myself and threw on some clothes, twisting my wet hair into a makeshift bun on top of my head. I raced downstairs calling for Zephaniah and Ned, but the ghosts were way ahead of me, and had already assembled in the bar.

I threw open the front door and dashed out onto the drive, Charity on my heels. Horses stood whinnying, and shaking their heads, harnesses jangling in the cool night air. Coachmen were alighting from the front of the carriages, and eerily silent, they assembled together at the head of the first group of horses. I walked forwards to greet them, fighting to contain the sudden onset of nerves. They turned as one to watch me advance, and I halted, shivers running down my spine.

I couldn't see their faces. Each of the coachmen hid behind a black leather mask, only their eyes glinted in the light from the gas lamps.

"Welcome to Whittle Inn," I said, swallowing my nerves.

One of the coachmen broke free of the others and held out a letter to me, written in red ink on the now familiar parchment. I broke the seal and moved into the light. It contained my orders for receiving the Laurent party. I read through the instructions quickly.

I was to arrange for the coffins to be stored in the beer cellar, where the vampires would remain during daylight hours. At night they wished to have use of their allotted rooms, and they insisted the bar and the kitchen remain open all though the hours of darkness. The coachmen would inspect the cellar for potential risks, then unload the coffins and store them safely.

My instructions were to stand by, and not allow my staff to interfere.

Charity and I looked on as the coachmen unloaded the coffins and took them around to the side of the inn, one by one, and manoeuvred them safely down the skids into the beer cellar. Methodically, as each hearse was vacated, it was led away and the one behind took its place.

Finally when all the coffins had been allocated a resting place, the head coachman tipped his hat at me and climbed aboard his hearse. He led his horses in a neat trot across the gravel drive and onto the lane, and then picked up speed. The others followed in well-ordered and impressive formation; dozens of the spookiest black horses I had ever encountered. I watched the blue gas lights go, until I could see them no longer, then I turned on my heel and walked back into the inn.

Charity raised her eyebrows and puffed her cheeks out.

I nodded at her. Now the real work would commence.

"Let's do this."

"By all the goddesses you scared me to death!" I shrieked.

Marc Williams became the first vampire to make it to the bar. "Hi," he said with a sheepish smile. "Sorry about that."

"Are you creeping around on purpose?" I scolded. "Are you trying to frighten us?"

"No," Marc protested. "I generally move this quietly. I think all vampires do. I used to be a clumsy oaf. Before."

I wanted to ask him about 'before' but didn't know how to broach it.

Charity laughed shakily. "Well that's going to take some getting used to. I had no idea you were there."

"How's the cellar?" I asked.

"Very nice. Cool and dark. A tad musty. Smells of old booze. Just the way I like it." Grinning, Marc inspected the optics and the bottles behind the bar. "Double malt? My favourite. I don't suppose ...?"

"Of course," I said. "That's what we're here for. I'll pour you a drink and then Charity can show you your room." I made the introductions. "Charity this is Marc. He's Melchior's best man. I've put you next door to Melchior, Marc. I trust that's okay?"

"Yes that's fine. I'll try and keep him out of trouble for you."

I blanched. "Will that be difficult?"

Marc shrugged. "Sometimes it's not that easy," he admitted.

I poured a double shot for Marc and a single

each for myself and Charity. I handed them each their glasses and held the whisky up to the light. It glittered rich and warm, highly symbolic of the hopes and dreams I had for my wonky hostelry.

"I now declare Whittle Inn open for business," I announced. "Cheers!"

My sense of achievement was short-lived to say the least.

Melchior made it upstairs from the cellar shortly after midnight. He had several hangers'-on in tow. An insolent young man in his early twenties, going by the name of Thaddeus Corinthian, who followed Charity around like a lap dog, smiling with a lascivious sneer every time she caught his eye, and two dark-haired vixens with cheekbones jutting out of their faces like mantlepieces, and sly eyes whom I firmly suspected of being the concubines Melchior had been sharing his bed with when I first encountered him in Hampstead.

It was difficult to tell now that I was seeing them fully-clothed.

I tried hard not to curl my lip every time I looked their way, but I have to admit, I found it difficult.

Sabien's appearance upstairs was somewhat of a relief. He at least, was unfailingly polite to both me and my staff—in fact most of the time I might even have stretched to calling him charming—however I sensed a dangerous side to him that I didn't want to discover further. He came over to introduce himself, standing just a little too close for comfort. He stood at around six feet, and where he might once have been dark haired, his hair was now a silvery grey. Like his son, his dress sense was impeccable, with beautifully cut Italian suits, and expensive shirts, worn with a silk cravat and solid gold cufflinks. In the muted lighting of the inn, his eyes seemed totally black, inky wells of oil, and while they glittered in the light, as with Melchior, there didn't appear to be much life within their depths.

"It eez so lovely to meet you, Alfhild," he said in his French accent, taking my hand and leaning over it, depositing a papery kiss from his pale lips on my knuckles. "I trust everything is in order for ze wedding proceedings?"

"It absolutely is," I replied brightly, "and if there are any problems at all, please do come and find me."

"You can be assured that I will," Sabien purred, holding on to my hand for far longer than was necessary. "I will track you down one way or another."

"Excellent." I didn't like the sound of that. I pulled my hand away, cringing inwardly. "Sabien, would you please excuse me for one moment while I just check everything is ready at the bar for our guests?" He bowed graciously, and I made my escape, aware of him staring after me as I walked away. The man was as predatory as his son.

It wasn't long before Melchior began to complain about a variety of things that were not to his liking. The wine hadn't been properly chilled, the—raw—meat hadn't been hung long enough. The inn was too brightly lit.

I passed his thoughts about the food on to Monsieur Emietter with some difficulty. My grandmama had disappeared and couldn't be found. I had a feeling she was intending to give the vampires a wide berth.

After I'd instructed the ghosts to turn down the lighting where possible, or switch off lamps where it wasn't, I found myself at a loss as how to meet Melchior's demands. There wasn't much I could do about the size or the age of the inn, and Melchior didn't like the room I had given him for some reason. It was the largest and grandest of all the guest bedrooms, but he complained that it was boxy –

which compared to his room at Laurent Towers I suppose was true enough.

He then professed a distaste for the furnishings – the suite was done out in oak - and insisted everything was replaced post-haste. When I explained that wouldn't be possible at this late stage, I thought he would bust a gut, his face reddening with fury, but his father placed a restraining hand on his arm, and Melchior smiled at me instead.

A smile that would crack solid ice.

I shuddered.

No wonder Gwyn had disappeared.

I spent the next hour or so trying to avoid Melchior and his father, while seeing to the other members of the party. Charity and I had our hands full though, and while Florence tried to help where she could, the vampires took exception to her charred scent, and kept requesting expensive bottles of cologne, that I of course, had not thought to get in.

I burned scented candles instead, and from time to time Charity sprayed air freshener as discreetly as possible, but again the vampires complained about the synthetic chemical scents drifting throughout the ground floor of the inn. Eventually, and reluctantly, I had no choice but to banish Florence to the kitchen to work on the wedding cake, while Zephaniah took her place helping me out in the bar.

Charity and I were run ragged attending to everyone's needs and given the early start we'd had, we hit the wall at around three in the morning. This seemed to be the time when the vampires were just getting going. Thaddeus turned on our music system and plugged in his phone, and soon the inn vibrated loudly to the sound of some rock group I had never heard before.

Worried about the volume, and knowing full well that sound can travel a long distance in the silence of the night, I rushed to turn it down. A chorus of disapproval met this decision, but I stood firm.

After some time Melchior and one of his dark-haired beauties headed for the front door. I tried to keep an eye on them from where I was stationed behind the bar, but they were quickly lost from my sight. With Zephaniah and Charity also busy, I had to trust Melchior was simply heading out for a walk in the grounds and wouldn't get up to anything untoward.

I closed the door to my own bedroom with an

exhausted groan just before six in the morning. Sabien had led his party back down the cellar forty minutes previously and I had been helping Florence and Charity clean up. There would be more deliveries within a few hours, and suddenly the thought of how little sleep I would be getting over the next few days made me wonder whether this would all be worth it.

I opened the window to allow Mr Hoo in. He alighted on the bed post, and snuggled his head into his mass of feathers, eyes closed in seconds. After a cursory brushing of my teeth, I flopped into bed and covered myself with my duvet, with the same result.

The sound of a delivery lorry in the drive woke me just over four hours later, bringing to mind the cavalcade of black horses I'd seen the night before. Bleary-eyed and groggy with lack of sleep, I sat bolt upright. Mr Hoo, unusually, was nowhere to be seen. I reached for my dressing gown and pulled it on, tying the cord tightly around my middle, and headed for the bathroom.

But I pulled up short at my bedroom door.

Tacked to the reverse of the door was a note. With hands trembling with a mix of fear, fury and loathing, I unpinned the note to read it. Melchior had issued further instructions. He wanted a private room to entertain his guests, and more armchairs in the bar area.

I glanced around my bedroom. My private space. The place I ran to when I needed to escape from everybody else. The only person I let in here was Gwyn, and only because it had once been her bedroom too and she seemed to think she had first dibs on it.

And Mr Hoo? Had he flown off when Melchior invaded our territory? The window was open. I always left it ajar while I slept. With any luck Mr Hoo had headed into Speckled Wood and was safely ensconced on a nice comfortable branch somewhere, well away from the vampires.

Melchior had been in my room while I'd slept.

You had to question how you could ever trust a man like that.

I knew for certain, I didn't.

CHAPTER ELEVEN

Once I'd attended to business around the inn I had to head down into Whittlecombe to Primrose Cottage. A house clearance firm were arriving to take away all the large items of furniture left in Derek's home, along with the boxes of pots and pans and kitchen utensils I had cleared from the kitchen. I'd already arranged for a few local charities to take his clothes, as well as tins of food and store cupboard items they could pass on to someone in need, so very little remained in the house now.

I waited outside, out of the way of the removal men, and Millicent Ballicott came out of her cottage to stand with me.

"You look pale." Jasper and Derek's little Yorkshire Terrier, Sunny, sniffed around my ankles.

"I feel totally washed out. I've had four hours

sleep and it's likely I won't get more than that in the next twenty-four hours either."

"What's going on? Problems at the inn?"

"You could say that. Or perhaps it's not a problem. Perhaps this is how my life will proceed from now on. With me lurching from one catastrophe with a guest to another."

Millicent's brow creased in concern. "What's up? Won't you be ready to open?"

"That's just it, Millicent," I said. "I'm already open. I accepted an invite to host a wedding at the inn. The ceremony takes place on the 31st but half of the guests have turned up early."

"Oh I see. Well I suppose it's good practice for you, for when you're open proper."

I laughed, but not with much humour. "I can't wait." I sounded fed up, and I hated to be the one to put a downer on life.

She cocked her head and regarded me more closely. I could see some amusement in her smile, but she looked puzzled too.

"This isn't like you, Alf."

The removal chaps chose that moment to exit the house, carrying a heavy armchair, the twin of the faded one I'd seen down the allotments in Derek's shed. Sunny lifted her head and scented the air and then turned her head as the men carried the chair past her, before crying and whining and pulling at her lead to go after them.

"Oh no!" I exclaimed. "How sad! She knows this is her master's chair."

Millicent bent down and picked the tiny dog up, while Jasper looked on petulantly, as if to say, *'why is she getting all the attention?'*

"Animals grieve too," Millicent said and snuggled the dog close.

"Did you know his wife Sarah?" I asked. Millicent had lived in Whittlecombe her whole life and had known my father and my grandparents.

"Yes. She was a lovely woman. Quiet. Mostly kept herself to herself. Well, they both did really. But she was a member of the WI and loved it there. Made some excellent gooseberry compotes as I recall."

The WI, or Women's Institute, was a quaint and—seemingly to my mind at least—old-fashioned group for women that had existed since the First World War. Its traditions were upheld here in the village with great fondness, and Millicent was a proud and fully-paid up member. She constantly invited me to join, but I was worried that even at the grand old age of thirty I'd be the youngest woman in attendance by about three decades.

No thanks.

"It's all very sad," I said. "What will happen to Sunny? Will you keep her?"

"I haven't really given it much thought. I'm not sure Jasper approves really. Poor Sunny is very needy and likes to get on my lap. Jasper is not getting as many snuggles as he usually does." Millicent held her out to me, and Sunny wagged her tail. "She likes you. Wouldn't you like a pet?"

"I think I have enough to deal with at the moment, Millicent!"

She tittered, but her smile faded as the door at the end cottage opened and a woman in her mid-to-late thirties came out, and stood on the pavement, her hands on her hips, her mouth drawn up in an unpleasant sneer, watching the removal men do their work.

"Good afternoon, Grace," Millicent called, and I waved and smiled too, remembering this was Grace Gretchen. Bob's daughter. She lived here with him, and her two young sons.

Grace, never one to live up to her name, scowled at us.

"You can't get rid of his stuff fast enough, can

you?" Her whole face was hard with a hostility I was largely unaccustomed to in Whittlecombe. Most of the villagers here were gracious and pleasant.

Millicent glanced at me, perhaps wondering whether I wanted her to interject, but I fixed a smile to my face myself and replied.

"I've been in touch with the next of kin, Ms Gretchen, and I'm following her instructions."

Grace shook her head, curling her lip in a sneer. "We know all about you big city folk here. You think you're one of us but you're not. You come down here with your fancy ways, selling off the land and now putting good folk out of their homes so you can flog the cottages off too. You're everything that's wrong with this country. You need to go back to where you came from."

I rocked back on my heels, hurt by how unfair her accusations were. That was the exact opposite of what I was trying to do. I tried to protest but she cut me off.

"And we know all about your dark ways and supernatural doings. You have us right where you want us, don't you?" She spun around, heading for her front door, but before she re-entered her cottage she spat one final stream of vitriol at me. "You can come after me if you want. With everything you've got. I'm not afraid of your sort, I can assure you of that!"

Rhona was on her own in the General Stores, although fortunately not busy, when I stepped into her shop, relieved to be away from the curtain-twitching neuroticism of Grace Gretchen at Dandelion Cottage.

"Hi Alf," Rhona greeted me, wiping her hands on her apron. "Have you gone down with it too?"

"Down with it? With what?"

"Some sort of virus. There seems to be a lot of it about. Stan's upstairs in bed. He looks like death. And I've sold out of cold and flu remedies. I've been inundated. I thought maybe you had what he has?"

I was sorry to hear Stan was poorly. "No, it's just a lack of sleep in my case," I said. "You know how it is. So much to do before the inn opens."

"Just a few days left. You must be excited?"

The bell over the shop door jangled behind me. A woman I barely knew came into the shop and marched up to the counter, pushing ahead of me. She pretty much looked how I felt.

"Hello, Claudia," Rhona said politely, looking

back at me to see if I minded. I shook my head and winked at her.

"Afternoon, Rhona. Do you have flu remedy? I'm coming down with something and I just can't afford to take time off work to stay in bed."

"I don't have anything left, Claudia. I'm so sorry. Stan has taken to his sick bed too, so I can't even send him to the wholesalers."

I grabbed a couple of lemons from Rhona's greengrocer's shelving section. "You could try ordinary painkiller with a hot lemon drink," I suggested, trying to be helpful. Claudia turned to look at me suspiciously. "I use that all the time. Crush the tablets. I add honey. Stir it up."

"Is that right?" The woman's eyes narrowed. "Is that some sort of witchy concoction?"

Taken aback, I shook my head. "You could throw in a shot of whisky too," I added quietly. "For a bit of a kick. It helps you sleep."

Claudia glared at me as though I had suggested grilling her firstborn after bleeding it dry, then sacrificing it to the King of Darkness. She twisted about and marched out of the shop without so much as a by-your-leave.

"Oof," I said when she had gone. Stunned to be

finding myself the cause of so much angst in the village, I couldn't help feeling extraordinarily hurt.

"What was that about?" Rhona asked, staring in confusion at Claudia's retreating back.

"I have no idea. I have never spoken to that woman before in my life."

"That was a genuinely useful idea, Alf," Rhona tried to console me. I had a feeling I was looking a little woebegone. "If anyone else comes in needing stuff for a cold, I'll try and sell them lemons."

"Go for it," I said, trying not to sound too grouchy. "Sometimes lemons are all that life gives you."

Chapter Twelve

I trudged wearily past Dandelion Cottage, imagining the curtains twitching and Gretchen's hostile eyes staring out at me, as I returned to the inn. Primrose Cottage stood nestled between its neighbours, looking increasingly sad and empty, the boarded-up window in the front bedroom a stark reminder to me of a danger that wouldn't go away, and one that seemed to lack explanation.

I found myself looking at the floor as I walked up Whittle Lane, my forehead wrinkled, my mood bleak. It seemed stupid to feel so cross and low, but I couldn't shake off the feeling of injustice from a few of my encounters in the village this afternoon. My arrival into Whittlecombe had been bumpy, to say the least, but overall I'd found the villagers more accepting of late—so what was all the aggro about?

By the time I arrived at the inn I had given

myself a good talking to. Think about it: you can't change the way other people view you, you can only change your thought patterns in relation to that. It shouldn't matter to me what Claudia and Grace thought of me. They were entitled to their own opinion.

They were rude though, I told myself. I didn't intend to stoop to their level.

I decided my over-tiredness was a contributing factor to my hyper-sensitivity. If everything was under control at the inn, perhaps I would take a nap for a few hours before it grew dark.

But thinking about my nocturnal guests made me feel even more gloomy, and I probably had a face like thunder when I walked through the door. Charity spotted my expression the second she clapped eyes on me as I joined her in the main bar. She was busily drying wine glasses and stacking them safely in place, ready for the evening. "Wooo," she exclaimed. "You need to get out more. It works wonders for lifting your whole demeanour!"

"No need for the sarcasm," I countered. "You wouldn't believe the afternoon I've had. What is wrong with people today? Is Florence around? I'm desperately in need of sustenance. Of the baked and sweet variety, preferably."

Charity shook her head. "Sorry, Alf. No time. We've had another guest arrive and more deliveries."

"Another guest?" I asked confused. "Are we expecting any more?"

"How about the bride?"

"The bride? Well, yes, of course. How could I forget?" I gestured at the window, slightly bewildered. "But it's daytime. Have they delivered her already?"

Charity's nod, over my shoulder, was virtually imperceptible.

I stopped talking, moving or even thinking. I simply froze. What did that nod mean?

I turned slowly, and there, sitting alone in one of the wing-backed armchairs by the fire, hugging herself and looking for all the world like a little lost waif, was a young woman. She had one battered suitcase and a modest brown leather handbag, and I couldn't help but think these were all the belongings she had in the entire world.

She was a sweet rose of a woman, early twenties, long undyed chestnut colour hair without a hint of curl, pale skin that glowed with good health, striking features—warm brown eyes, full lips, a roman nose—and when I walked towards her and she stood to greet me, I could see that she was tall, maybe five foot ten or eleven, but so slender, she could have been a model.

"Hello," I said holding my hand out. "Welcome to Whittle Inn. I'm Alf Daemonne."

"Hi, Alf," she replied, her voice as sweet as her countenance, and her English excellent but her accent pronounced. "Ekaterina Lukova. I'm pleased to finally arrive here and to meet you. You can call me Kat if you like."

I looked her up and down, and then glanced back at Charity who shrugged. We were both thinking the same thing. She didn't look like a vampire. She seemed far too alive and vital for that. The blush on her cheeks was entirely natural.

"You're earlier than we thought you would be. The ...ah ... rest of the wedding guests appear by night." I have no idea why I felt the need to pussy-foot around her. She was the bride. She had to know what she was doing.

When she didn't respond, I continued, curious to know more about her. "Where are you from?"

"I'm from a little town in Russia called Chernoistochinsk. This place, Whittlecombe? It reminds me a little of it, I think. Countryside. Fields. Trees. I think I am homesick already."

Florence appeared with a tray of tea and cake,

and a jug of water. She set it on the occasional table next to Ekaterina's chair. I pulled up a nearby stool.

"Have you come here by yourself?"

Ekaterina hesitated. "Yes. My mama, she is… busy… and you know, the air fare? It is expensive."

Expensive? I bit my tongue. Surely Sabien could have coughed up the cash to get Ekaterina's mother over here. He was loaded.

"Where do you live when you're in England?" I asked,

Kat tipped her head and smiled. "This is my first time in UK, Alf. I've only ever seen your country in films and on the TV."

I must have looked shocked because the young Russian woman tipped her head back and laughed. I watched, smiling. My goodness, she was astoundingly beautiful.

A thought crept into my head, and I couldn't help myself, I had to ask, "But you have met Melchior before, right?"

Kat stopped laughing and looked serious. "Yes, yes. We have met several times."

But not dated? Not walked in the rain or skinny-dipped in a river? Not spent saucy weekends in a cabin in the countryside? I wanted to probe further, find out more about how they had come to be a couple, and fallen in love. But I couldn't. I wasn't aware of the etiquette with vampires and the customs surrounding their betrothals.

"Are you looking forward to the big day?" I asked instead, and Kat smiled, a genuine grin of delight. "Oh yes. Melchior is so handsome. I know we will have the time of our lives. It will be a beautiful wedding. He promised that."

I poured tea and offered her a cup, then indicated the cake. One of Florence's wonderful chocolate sponges, but Kat shook her head. "Oh no, thank you," she replied. "I daren't put an ounce on. I've been dieting so hard. Melchior was very specific about the weight I should be and the measurements I must make."

I almost choked on the forkful of cake I was chewing on. "He told you what you should weigh? That seems incredibly controlling."

Kat shrugged, her eyes giving nothing away. "No. I don't think so. He is supplying the dress and everything that goes with it. If it doesn't fit it will be a disaster." She laughed again, but this time, to my ears, it echoed with a hollow ring.

"We've had to do a great deal by long distance, so trusting each other, it is so important."

"Mm," I said, recalling finding Melchior at home

with the two dark-haired beauties in his pseudo-Greek full-on-bad-taste bedroom. "Yes, you're right there. Trust is important."

"I would never want to let Melchior down. I will be the perfect wife," Kat continued, her eyes wide and artless, but it sounded like a script to my suspicious mind.

From behind the bar Charity was gesturing at me fiercely. I tried to ignore her, but she kept on. When I fully looked her way she tilted her head and tapped her neck. I threw her a warning look and refocused on Kat.

"Where do you intend to live when you're married?" Laurent Towers in Hampstead, Melchior's current habitat wouldn't suit this sweet young woman at all.

"I'll leave that all in Melchior's capable hands," she opined, her voice as smooth as caramel.

I abandoned my cake, feeling like I might be overdosing on sugar somewhere along the line. "Why don't I show you to your room? It's on the floor above Melchior's. I thought I'd keep the bride and groom separate." I'd done that for tradition, now I wondered whether I might actually be saving her life. "Is this all the luggage you have?"

"Yes," Kat said, as I bent to pick up her case.

There was no weight to it, it might have been empty. As someone who needed a huge case for a quick weekend away, this appeared strange. "Melchior promised he would buy me all I need, when I need it." Her voice was soft and sincere, and I felt afraid for her. Melchior was playing games with this naïve young woman's life. Here she was so far from home without a friend or her mother to accompany her. It seemed totally wrong to me.

I couldn't help it, in the end I simply blurted out the question both Charity and I were dying to ask, "You know what he is, don't you?"

"Yes of course," she said, turning to give me the full benefit of her glittering green eyes, soft and dreamlike. "I know what Melchior is."

Unlike her betrothed, Kat seemed entirely content with the room I had given her. This one had been painted the palest of blues, with linen as white as snow. Then Charity had come along and added some splashes of a gorgeous sea-green with a throw, rug and a couple of scatter cushions. The paintings on the wall in this room, were seaside scenes of nearby Durscombe. One showing the red cliffs, the other, fishermen and their wives congregating outside The Blue Bell Inn waiting for news after a ship wreck.

I left Kat in her room to relax and made my way downstairs to finish off my tea. My cake lay where I had discarded it and I caught Florence giving me a hurt glance, probably thinking I hadn't enjoyed her cake, which couldn't have been further from the truth.

Charity waylaid me when I carried the tray back into the kitchen where Monsieur Emietter was cutting up what looked like a whole cow on the main work surface and Florence was prepping vegetables. "Well?" she demanded.

"Well what?" I asked innocently.

"You know what," Charity hissed. "She—Ekaterinaburg or whatever her name is—doesn't look anything like a vampire."

"She likes to be called Kat. I don't think she can be one, can she? She's just too... alive."

"So what then?" Charity asked, her voice full of incredulity. Monsieur Emietter shot us a look loaded with daggers. "She's normal like us—well me at any rate—and she's going to marry Melchior?"

"It would appear so." I deposited my dirty dishes by the sink and Monsieur Emietter scowled at me.

"We can't let that happen, Alf. It's like sending a lamb to the slaughter!"

"Well what do you suggest we do?" I asked, feeling helpless in the face of her passionate onslaught. "I can't get in the middle of this."

"Well why on earth not? This isn't an episode of Star Trek. You don't have a Prime Directive."

"A prime wha—?"

"Never mind. Alf. Seriously. Does she even know what she's letting herself in for? Are we going to be responsible for turning her into some kind of... monster?"

And there we had it. The problem in a nutshell. A clash of cultures. A clash of supernatural beings if you like.

"Charity," I said slowly, miserably. "If I was—or we were—to wade in between Melchior and Kat, what would that say about me? About us? I'm a witch. My kind have been persecuted for millennia. And that's the same for Melchior, Sabien and the rest."

"But you don't hurt people," Charity was so angry now she almost stamped her foot.

"I don't. My coven don't. We live by the precepts, 'hurt none' and 'do only good', but that's not the same for all covens and for all witches. There are bad as well as good."

"But you," Charity wagged her finger at me, her face as pink as her hair, "you don't. You don't hurt anyone, and you don't groom people and turn them into witches. But that's exactly what Melchior is doing here, surely?"

I could see her point of view, and there was no way I wanted anyone to get hurt, but as far as I could tell from our admittedly limited conversations thus far, Kat was here of her own free will, and to my knowledge she was an adult who seemed to know what she was doing. I was being paid to provide a service. Here at Whittle Inn we just had to host the wedding.

Didn't we?

If I'd thought the previous evening had been bad, this night took the proverbial biscuit.

Right from his appearance soon after the moon had risen, just after eight, I could tell Melchior was in a foul mood. He seemed intent on drinking everyone else under the table, so I kept a careful eye on how much he was putting away, and as soon as I could corner Marc I did so.

"Can't you rein Melchior in a little?" I asked, and he followed the direction of my gaze. Melchior was sitting with one of his dark-haired beauties, plying her with red wine. "Kat arrived this afternoon and she's upstairs now. I don't want her to come down and find him dancing on the tables with one of his ..." I was lost for words for a moment, then tried, "floozies."

Marc laughed good naturedly.

"Ekaterina is here, is she?" His face lit up. "Thank goodness she's arrived safely. I ought to let Melchior know." We both glanced over again. Melchior appeared to be having a heated discussion with Thaddeus, who was gesticulating wildly. Marc watched them, his face inscrutable. He didn't make a move to go over and tell Melchior that Kat was here.

"Marc," I said, pulling his attention back to me. "About Kat. She isn't a vampire, is she?"

Marc studied me, his eyes thoughtful. Then, reluctantly, he shook his head. "No. She's not."

I waited.

"Do you think it's wrong?" Marc fiddled with his glass, swirling the remains of tonic and lemon round the bottom.

I shrugged. "I don't think it's my place to judge, but..." I puffed my cheeks out. "It's certainly hard to understand."

"But if she loves him?" His voice was soft, so quiet I could hardly hear him.

"Then I say let it be."

Marc nodded and drained his glass. "So do I."

Kat chose that moment to make her entrance. She descended gracefully down the stairs, wearing white skinny jeans, and a lightweight blue and white jumper. She had washed her hair, and it hung down her back, soft and fluffy and gleaming like angels' wings. She looked casual but smart at the same time.

"Wow," I said, and Marc stood next to me, both of us gazing in admiration.

One by one, everyone in the room noticed Kat and there were whoops and hollers and cat calls. Several people applauded her as she moved down the stairs smiling sweetly at everyone and waving timidly to a few people she knew. In turn, Melchior's dark-haired beauties smiled up at her, and made all the right welcoming noises, but their eyes smouldered with resentment.

It didn't matter. Kat seemed to have plenty of fans, including Sabien, who walked over to the stairs, where Kat had paused for effect. He offered his hand which she took, and elegantly stepped down into the bar. Her father-in-law bent close to her and whispered in her ear. She emitted a musical laugh and he smiled back at her in evident delight.

Only Melchior seemed entirely unmoved by his bride-to-be's arrival. For sure, he smiled along with everyone else, but I observed him as he approached her, with his usual swagger, and I didn't need my witchy sixth-sense to see there was an evident distance between them.

He leaned in to kiss her cheek as his father had done before, but instead of enveloping her in a welcoming hug, or saying something to make her smile into his eyes, he pulled back and I distinctly heard him say, "Really, Ekaterina. You couldn't have worn something a little more sophisticated than this? And have you lost any weight at all?"

I held my breath, hoping she would put the presumptive little monster in his place, but she simply moved her head slightly, as though frightened his words would hurt her, and avoided his gaze.

"Take a seat by the fire," he instructed with a snap. "We'll discuss the order of events later."

She did as she was told and sat largely alone for the next few hours. Occasionally Marc or Sabien would wander over and make conversation, and I would watch her face lift. Then their attention would be called upon by Thaddeus, Melchior or one of the rest of the party and she would nod graciously as they took their leave. For my part I went over and offered her a drink from time to time in between looking after everyone else, but on the whole, she appeared isolated from this crowd she would soon be such a central part of.

I felt bad for her, and when sometime after one in the morning I looked up from serving drinks and Melchior and his vixens had disappeared leaving Kat to it, I went over and suggested she go up to bed.

I thought she would refuse, perhaps make an excuse for the behaviour of her fiancé, but when she met my eyes I found fiery indignation there—in the set of her jaw and the line of her lips—and she nodded. "Good idea. I am tired after my long journey. I would like to see more of Vittlecombe in the morning."

I smiled at her accent. "Yes! You should head down into the village and talk to Rhona in the general stores, or Gloria in the café. Some of the villagers will be here for your wedding. I'm sure they would love to meet you."

"They will be here? Melchior invited them?"

"No, no," I replied. *As if.* "It's the official re-opening of the inn and I was already having a party that evening, so quite a few of the locals have been invited here, and they'll be delighted to watch your nuptials. It will be quite a spectacle for them."

"I'm sure it will," Kat cooed.

Chapter Thirteen

It took a litre of coffee before I could properly wake up the following day. I noticed that Charity, who normally opted for minimal make-up was wearing a thick layer of concealer. We sat together at the kitchen table, nibbling on toast, checking where we were with everything, creating lists of things that still needed doing, and assigning ghosts—and each other—to the various tasks.

Out in the main bar area, and in The Snug and The Nook, the Wonky Inn Clean-up Crew led by Florence were hard at it, deep cleaning after yet another night of wild shenanigans. The vampires certainly knew how to party. There was every chance I was going to have to refurbish the downstairs of the inn with new curtains, rugs and cushions once they had left. Spillages and stains were everywhere.

"I look like death," Charity complained when I remarked upon her appearance.

I tapped my own eye-bags gently with my fingers. "Me too. But this will be the first time the inn will have made any money since I took over. Think of that! And I'll owe you a fortune in overtime."

Charity growled at me.

"No? Okay, well, in that case, just do what I do and forward think."

"What is that when it's at home? Forward thinking?"

I sat back and rearranged my features into something I hoped approximated blissful calm, and held my arms loosely out in front of myself, touching middle finger to thumb. "Oh you know, you tell yourself 'it's *only* 61 hours and thirty-three minutes to the wedding and then I can have my life back'."

"Oh I see." Charity observed the way I was sitting with a slight curl of her lip and thought about what I'd said. "Does that work? I suppose it helps. It doesn't make the situation seem so bad. How long is it until the wedding?

"Sixty-one hours and thirty-three minutes."

Charity burst out laughing. "You're already counting?"

I dropped my hands and laughed along with her.

"I totally am! And listen to this. I'm also thinking, for more than 32 of those hours, Melchior and his hell-bound horde will be safely tucked up in their earth filled coffins. I call that positive forward thinking, don't you?"

"You're not enjoying their company I take it?"

I shook my head seriously. "Gwyn hasn't been seen since the hearses arrived, and Mr Hoo disappeared out of my room the other night and I haven't seen him either. I've been fretting about him."

"He's probably hiding out in the woods until all this is over."

Lucky Mr Hoo. "I wish I could do that."

"He'll be back."

"I hope so. I miss the little wobbly-headed dude." I sighed.

Charity smiled warmly and patted my arm. "Stop worrying. You're doing a great job, boss lady,"

"Right back at ya, minion." I winked at her, feeling warm in our close companionship.

Charity giggled again. "More coffee, Alf?"

How could I refuse?

George Gilchrist phoned a little later, and I smiled to hear his voice.

"Keeping busy?" he asked.

"Unbelievably busy. And sleep is at a premium."

"Join the club." I heard his laugh, he sounded tired too. "I've lost count of the amount of overtime I've done in the past two weeks. I'm developing a nervous twitch."

He said it with humour, but I couldn't help worrying. "That doesn't sound too good."

"No. I could do with a break, that's for sure." He took a deep breath. "Listen, Alf, you've been emptying the cupboards at Derek Pearce's house, haven't you?"

"Dandelion Cottage? Yes."

"You haven't found any traces of any other chemicals anywhere?"

I hadn't. The house had been relatively clutter free. "No. Even the shed in the garden was empty."

"Completely empty?"

"Yes." He was quiet on the other end of the phone. "Do you find that odd?" I certainly did. *Who keeps absolutely nothing in the shed?*

"I do." George was hesitant.

"What's up?"

"The forensics came back on the chemicals from

the shed, and in themselves they're relatively innocuous although not really that type of thing you want to be sprinkling on your potato patch. It doesn't sit right that Derek was storing them at the allotment, that's my gut instinct."

"I see," I said, biting my lip. Curious. "What about a cause of death?"

"Inconclusive. Broken neck, but no other injuries."

Poor Derek. What had gone on at Dandelion Cottage? And what was the link with The Mori?

I desperately wanted some answers but tied up here at the inn with this wedding, I was hard pushed for time.

"Alf?" George's voice interrupted my thoughts and he sounded as troubled as I felt. "You take care, okay?"

Late in the morning, deliveries began arriving once more, keeping Charity and I busy for most of the day. The sun had started to dip in the sky when the ring of the doorbell announced yet another. This one turned out to be two huge cardboard boxes, both marked fragile, addressed to Ekaterina. The first of these stood nearly six feet tall, although fortunately it was only one foot wide and one foot deep.

I recruited Zephaniah and Ned and with their help, Charity and I transported the bulky parcels upstairs to Kat's room. She had disappeared into the village for most of the middle part of the day, and taken her lunch at the café, enjoying a Devonshire cream tea at Gloria's urging, and then returned to the inn to nap.

I knocked quietly on the door, hoping she was awake. "Come," she called almost immediately and when I poked my head around the door I found her curled up on the window seat, reading some magazines she had purchased in Whittle Stores.

"Hi Kat, sorry to disturb you," I said. "We've had a few deliveries addressed for you. I have a feeling these may well be your wedding outfit!" Despite my misgivings about Kat and Melchior's relationship, I couldn't help feeling excited about seeing the wedding dress.

Kat jumped up with a grin and rushed over to help us get the boxes in. There wasn't a huge amount of space in the room for three women, two large boxes, a double bed and two ghosts but we managed. Then I ushered Zephaniah and Ned out ahead of me, but Kat called me back.

"Could you ladies help me do you think?" Kat asked. "The boxes are heavy, and I don't want to damage anything."

"Of course. We'd love to," Charity jumped in before I could say a word, and we carefully helped Kat peel back the layers of parcel tape that had been wrapped around the boxes. Inside the largest box was a makeshift wardrobe, and a plastic wrapped dress that hung from a rail.

Working together, we carefully lifted the dress from the rail and lay it down, plastic and all, on the bed. Charity ran to my office to fetch some scissors and then she very carefully slit open the plastic, and pulled the layers aside, so we could get a closer look at the frock.

As she stepped back, the three of us uttered a collective gasp.

Although I was taken aback by the colours, I don't think I had ever seen anything quite as magnificent. The dress was predominantly black but with a corseted bodice that gleamed in bright red satin. The skirt appeared to have a gathering behind it, rather like a bustle from the old days, and fell in stepped layers of black silk over a black satin underskirt. On the edging of every layer of the skirt, tassels created from tiny black beads had been attached, guaranteed to catch the light as the person wearing the dress moved. Similarly, the bodice of the dress was criss-crossed with strings of black beads, hanging in arcs like an extravagant necklace, falling from the low-cut neckline.

When we carefully turned the dress over, the rear of it had been similarly elaborately laced and decorated. The whole thing weighed a tonne.

In the bottom of the huge package were several black lace petticoats. Charity plucked one out and inspected it. "These look like they've been hand made," she marvelled. "I've never seen lace as beautifully worked as this.

"It's all exquisite." I breathed in wonder, running my fingers over the fabric, slightly envious.

"It wouldn't surprise me at all, if Melchior had arranged for all of this to be handmade. He's very generous," Kat said, stroking the satin bodice.

With Sabien's money, I thought.

"I'd like to try it on. Would you ladies help me?" Kat asked and without batting an eyelid began pulling off her clothes.

It was definitely a two-or-three-woman job. Getting into the petticoats was easy enough, but after that, the sheer weight and complexity of the dress made for some challenging moments. Buttons, hooks and eyes, and lacing—all were relentlessly fiddly, and I noted my fingers—totally lacking in nimbleness—were better at sanding doors than attending to such fine detail. Fortunately for me, Charity was unfailingly patient and had marvellous dexterity. I was reduced to the role of observer, and utterer of helpful phrases such as 'perhaps that one ties there?' and 'that seems a little loose' and 'Oh, that one's snagged' and 'you've missed a hook-and-eye there'.

When Kat was finally dressed, Charity and I stood in awe while she twisted and turned—with some difficulty it had to be said—in front of the wardrobe mirror, the dress rustling and jangling as she shifted. It was a stunning work of art, and it fitted like a glove, as though it had been moulded to the shape of Kat's body. She looked incredible but at the same time, the sheer weightiness of it, and its tight fit, prevented much in the way of movement. Kat was a prisoner in a wedding dress that she could neither get on nor take off by herself. It struck me that this was one more way that Melchior had control of her.

"You look incredible." Charity beamed at Kat.

Kat smoothed the skirts down and caught my eye in the mirror. Perhaps she recognised my thoughts from my expression because she frowned.

Charity's stomach rumbled, and I looked up in surprise. Outside it was full dark.

"I do beg your pardon, Kat," Charity said. "We skipped lunch today because we ate a late breakfast."

Kat looked horrified. "Oh my goodness. I am so sorry to have kept you. You should go and eat."

"The others will be up soon," I said. "I ought to make sure the bar is ready. I can't leave Florence on her own down there." *Not with Melchior constantly complaining about her smell.*

"Go, go!" Kat urged.

Charity glanced at me. "There's the other box."

"That will be the headdress," Kat said. "It can wait for now. My head won't have changed shape or size."

"Let's get you out of this and make you more comfortable," Charity said just as someone tapped hesitantly at the door.

We all froze. "Who is it?" I called.

"Marc."

The vampires were starting to rise. I needed to make a move.

I glanced back at Kat and she nodded, so I opened the door a crack.

Marc smiled apologetically. "Alf, I'm so sorry to bother you…" Behind us Kat was trying to manoeuvre the heavy frock around the bed and had snagged in some parcel tape.

Charity shouted, "Whoa," and Marc's eyes flicked to Kat behind me, and widened in surprise.

"Wow."

I was surprised at the flatness of his tone. "That's what we said." I made an attempt to sound enthusiastic. "You are alone, aren't you?"

Marc nodded, his expression grim. "Melchior is still in the cellar. That's an incredible dress." He didn't mean it as a compliment.

"She looks amazing doesn't she?" Charity called, not picking up on his mood. "Now away with you please."

I stepped out of the room, closing the door firmly behind me. "I'll come down with you now. I have some things to do. I'm sure Charity can manage by herself."

Marc stood and gazed at the door, his expression difficult to read. "Marc?" I prompted when he didn't immediately follow me.

"Sorry," he said and turned to me. I led the way down the corridor to the stairs and started down them. Marc paused again, looking back.

"Are you alright?" I asked. "You wanted me for something."

Marc stared at me in confusion, as though he had forgotten what he had been searching for. "I did, yes. It's not important though."

Now it was my turn to look puzzled. What was up with the man? He was normally so easy-going and smiley. Something appeared to have upset him. "Don't you like the dress?" I asked.

"It's hideous," he responded coldly, and stalked away from me.

Chapter Fourteen

An undercurrent of tension buzzed in the air of the bar that evening. Part of the problem, of course, was that it's entirely possible to become bored with people you are cooped up with for hours at a time, especially when you're having to do the same things over and over. I couldn't know how the vampires spent their leisure time under normal circumstances and in their own dwellings, but here at the inn, facilities were limited. In their places, I might have become a little bored too. Their only interests lay in drinking, carousing and playing loud music.

However tonight, the vampires had finally had enough of their hedonistic partying. Numerous squabbles broke out among them while I was managing the bar. Even before Kat made it back downstairs, Melchior's dark-haired twin vixens, were at each other's throats, slapping, biting and scratching. I looked up just in time to witness one of them sending a bottle flying. It smashed into one of my freshly decorated white walls, the red liquid staining the wall like watery blood, while Melchior stood back, roaring with laughter, and Thaddeus egged the women on.

Quick as a flash I was round the other side of the bar, "*Viscosi!*" I cried and all the glasses and bottles in the room, that weren't already being held in someone's hands, stuck to a surface. I was having no more spilled drinks and broken glass thank you very much.

But that was the easy part.

I ran over to attempt to separate the women, and eventually with Marc and Charity's help, did manage to split them up. I sent one of them into The Nook with Marc to cool down, and the other licked her wounds in Sabien's company.

"What was all that about?" I asked Charity, but she didn't know either.

"Jealousy, I reckon," she said, nodding up at Kat who was just making an entrance.

"You could be right." My eyes remained fixed on the remaining vixen who now extricated herself from Sabien's party and wandered over to give Melchior a shoulder massage. He peered up at her, standing behind him and patted her hand. They both watched Kat as she swept across the bar, seemingly oblivious to Melchior and his companion, to chat with Charity and myself.

"Thank you so much for helping me earlier."

"It was our pleasure," Charity gushed. I could see she was a complete sucker for weddings. This was good news if Whittle Inn was ever to host any more in the future.

If I ever got over this one.

"We're at your service should you need us the day after tomorrow," I offered.

"I will certainly need help." Kat nodded, eyes wide. "The dress is so complex."

"The dress has arrived, has it, my sweet?" Melchior appeared from nowhere and gripped Kat's upper arm so tightly, I could see where he was leaving dents in her skin.

"It has, my love." Kat half-turned to regard her betrothed. How she was resisting yanking her arm away from him, I couldn't comprehend. "It is as beautiful as you promised it would be. Charity and Alf have offered to help me dress on our special day. Isn't that kind of them?"

"Oh it is. Indeed it is." Melchior turned to fix me with his cold dead eyes. *Back off*, he was saying, I could hear the words loud and clear. I smiled at him through gritted teeth. "Very kind. But there's no need. I have a woman who can help you, my love. An expert in make-up too. You don't need to worry about a thing. Alfhild and Chastity will be able to carry on with their own duties. They will have more than enough to do."

"Charity," Charity retorted, bristling in indignation. I put a hand out and rubbed her back.

"We're here for you, whatever you need," I replied to Melchior and smiled at Kat. "Whenever you need it."

The next ruckus involved Thaddeus and a vampire I hadn't had much to do with so far, although he always seemed to be in the thick of what was happening. He was a handsome young man by the name of Gorkha, who was notable for his laugh. He sounded like a deranged hyena.

Afterwards, I could never be sure exactly what kicked it off, or who started what. Marc had returned from The Nook in search of another shot of whisky and had perched on a stool at the bar. The general noise levels in the lounge bar had risen to those I was rapidly becoming used to: louder than I was particularly comfortable with, but not so loud that my nearest neighbours would be calling the police to complain about the noise nuisance. But the tone of the merriment had changed. What was normally good-humoured banter, raucous singing, some jeering and a bit of argy-bargy, had become something that was simultaneously fiery and hostile.

I looked up from serving Marc to see Thaddeus and Gorkha circling the room, eyes fixed on each other. Melchior was gesticulating dramatically to Thaddeus, who held a hand up to him, to close him off. This one gesture seemed to particularly rankle Melchior. He tipped his head slightly to one side, his eyes burning like charcoal and said something in a low voice that I couldn't hear.

This time Thaddeus looked his way abruptly, and Melchior spoke to him again. Thaddeus deflated like a punctured balloon and all the fight left him. He slumped and held his hands up in appeasement to Melchior who grinned good-naturedly and held his own hands out to his friend.

But Gorkha wouldn't let it drop. He cat-called Melchior, called him a coward, and loudly declared to the by now hushed bar that Thaddeus was merely Melchior's pet, with no free will of his own.

Thaddeus tipped his head back and exposed his throat, laughing loudly, and in return calling Gorkha a foolish child. This lit the torch paper, and suddenly vampires were flying around the room. Faster than a speeding bullet, Thaddeus had Gorkha pinned to the floor with one hand around his neck, his eyes filled with blood and his fangs more pronounced than I'd seen before.

Beside me Charity shrieked and clutched her hands to her face.

"I could rip your throat out, boy!" Thaddeus screamed into the younger vampire's face.

I rushed around to the other side of the bar, but Marc grabbed my arm and held me back. "No," he hissed, his voice quiet enough so that only I could hear. "I won't be able to help you if you get involved. Stay back. Please."

I tried to pull free, but Marc was strong.

The vampires closed the circle around Thaddeus and Gorkha, and for the first time I could really see them for the predators they were, stalking their prey with calm, cold alacrity. Fixated, aggressive, merciless.

"Don't let them," I said to Marc, trying to rip my arm free, but he only shook his head.

Just when I thought all was lost for Gorkha,

Sabien called the vampires off and then stalked through the circle to stand next to Thaddeus. He tapped the young man on the shoulder, who in turn relaxed his grip of Gorkha's throat and slowly moved away.

As suddenly as it had started, it was all over.

Gorkha hopped to his feet and with a wry smile straightened his clothes. Then he walked out of the front door of the inn with one of the smirking vixens.

Marc released me with an apology. "I couldn't let you get hurt," he said miserably, and headed over to join Melchior.

With my knees wobbling a little, I cleaned up some glasses and plates and joined Charity behind the bar. "I don't know how much more of these people I can put up with," I whispered to her. "They're turning my hair grey."

Charity checked the clock on the wall behind us. "Forty-one hours and 52 minutes. And counting."

I had the makings of a cracking headache, and for one awful second considered whether I was the latest victim of whatever virus had hit Whittlecombe, until I figured stress and lack of sleep were most likely to blame.

I turned my attention to a guest waiting at the bar, but observed Kat over his shoulder, sitting alone next to the fire, watching Melchior with the same inscrutable expression I'd seen her wearing so many times before.

But this time, I swear I saw her lip curl.

Marc spent most of the evening trying to soothe things over with Thaddeus and Gorkha, and by the early hours it did appear as though we were getting somewhere. The vampires had calmed down, they were less raucous, and seemed capable of chatting pleasantly. From time to time, one or more would exit the inn and I could only assume they were visiting the portable blood bank they had brought with them.

What this blood bank actually was, I can't say, and I didn't like to think about it too much. It had arrived on the same evening as the vampire cavalcade and I'd had it positioned at the side of the inn, close by the entrance to the cellar. From then on I had tried to ignore its presence, and I hadn't ventured inside. Some things are not for me to see.

From outside it looked like a Portaloo, although coloured silver and made of stainless steel rather than heavy duty plastic. It measured approximately six feet square, large enough to allow one vampire to enter and be serviced—in whatever form that took. A vampire would step in, remain inside for some time, and then when they ventured back outside, they tended to look a little less peaky—not quite so corpse-like—and they were generally more even-tempered.

The final few hours of the night before the dawn, were quiet. For the first time, I saw a glimmer of civilisation among my guests. I overheard them chatting about the portraits on the wall, and then about artists some of them had known—Sabien claimed to have met Leonardo da Vinci—and paintings they had owned—Thaddeus, back to his usual braying self, bragged he had a Van Gogh in his Paris home.

"Do you believe him?" Charity asked, eyebrows raised, as we wiped down the bar and prepared to shut up shop for the night. Clearing the glasses and buffet could wait until we'd managed a few hours of shut-eye.

I regarded Thaddeus with glazed vision. "Who knows with this bunch? Vampires can live ridiculously long lives. Many claim to be immortal."

"Eww. Would you like to live forever?" Charity asked.

I shook my head. "Just long enough to see the back of this bunch."

Charity guffawed, and we watched the vampires drift away. We headed to our own bedrooms just before six.

Perhaps, at last, I was becoming somewhat accustomed to the ridiculous hours I was keeping, but when I awoke later that morning, after four and half hours sleep, I felt a little more optimistic about the day ahead. Or perhaps it was the knowledge that when I awoke in 48 hours' time, this whole nightmare would be over, and I could make inroads into attracting a better kind of clientele.

Football hooligans, University freshers, and out-of-control hen parties would be a cinch after this.

With a grunt, I rolled out of bed, grabbed my robe and headed to the window. I leaned out and breathed in the fresh balmy air, checking for signs of Mr Hoo. Nothing. Despite the brilliant sunshine of the morning, I could tell by the feel of the breeze that we were in for some rain. I made a mental note to check the weather forecast. A slight shower or two this afternoon wouldn't be a problem, and certainly after such a long dry summer and autumn, the grounds could do with a sprinkling, but heavy rain would really put a dampener on proceedings the following day.

We had a marquee on stand-by, but I was pretty sure Melchior would not be best pleased if we had to resort to that.

There are many things I can control, but the weather is not one of them.

I made my way downstairs to find that I was first up. Yawning, I set the kettle to boil and wandered down the back passage of the inn, checking on the condition of The Snug and The Nook—not too bad—then opened the frosted glass door and entered the bar. The room was in complete darkness which was unusual. Someone had pulled the shutters tight and drawn the curtains. Neither Charity nor I had done so when we called it a night a few hours previously.

Rather than stumble around in the darkness, I tried to switch the lights from the central panel by the door. Nothing happened.

"Looks like we've lost our electricity in here," I mused aloud and called for Zephaniah. I'm happy to turn my hand to most things. But plumbing and electricity? They're best left to the experts. Not that Zephaniah was an expert himself by any means. Electricity had been in its infancy while he was alive.

I heard someone coming down the front stairs.

"Is that you Alf?" Charity called. "It's dark in here, isn't it? Shall I put the lights on?"

"Try that side." I fumbled around near the till. I knew I had a torch somewhere. I could hear Charity flipping switches.

"Oh that's odd," I heard her mumbling.

"I think we must have some sort of electrical short." I called for Zephaniah again.

"Bear with me then." Her voice drifted closer. "I'll open the shutters." A few seconds later she collided with a table and cursed.

"Mind how you go," I said and smiled. My hand closed around the torch at last and I flicked it on. It didn't give off much light. The battery was failing. "Shall I light your way?" I asked and swung the torch around to catch Charity as she pulled the curtains open and reached for the blinds.

But the limited amount of light also caught something else. A person on the large wing back armchair which had been moved from its habitual place by the fire to the very centre of the floor.

"Who's that?" I asked and stepped towards them, just as Charity flung open the shutters to let the sun in.

And in that split second of time, I knew. I shrieked and launched myself forwards, trying to block the light, or prevent the inevitable, but I was too late.

Even as I hurled myself into the air in front of him, and Charity spun to find out why I had shrieked, Thaddeus, gagged by masking tape, and tied securely to the armchair was hit full in the face by the sun's rays. He kicked his legs. His arms—taped to the thick arm rests—juddered in panic as his skin shrivelled and crisped like a burned jacket potato. His eyes, at first wide and petrified, turned white as he was rapidly blinded. He gazed around himself in blank horror for the tiniest fraction of a second, and then in the next instant, he imploded and became dust where he sat. Motes of who he'd been, swirled about in the sunlight around me as I tumbled to the floor, Charity's scream, a siren in my head.

Chapter Fifteen

What could I have done?

What could Charity have done?

Someone had tied Thaddeus to that chair, and shorted the electricity in the bar area, knowing full well that the first thing we would do when we came downstairs would be to open the shutters.

It occurred to me now, as I walked into the village—not so much because I needed anything but just because I was desperate to get out of the inn, away from the guests who slept like the dead—that whomever had waylaid Thaddeus and tied him to the chair, had been cutting it all a bit fine. Charity and I had only gone to our rooms when every last one of the guests had called it a night. A faint slither of light could be seen on the horizon when I pulled my curtains. Dawn would have been swift.

The murderer—if that's what he or she was,

because how do you murder someone who essentially ceased to exist a very long time ago—was a risk taker, that much was clear. I remembered the fight between Gorkha and Thaddeus earlier in the evening. Gorkha had to be the prime suspect, but Melchior was the one I mistrusted the most. I had to leave it for now, because I could hardly march down into the cellar and demand answers. That would have to wait until this evening.

So lost in my thoughts was I, I almost knocked over the elderly Mr Bramble as I walked past his cottage. He was pruning his hedge.

"I do beg your pardon, Mr Bramble," I said. "I was miles away."

He waved me away, holding a handkerchief to his mouth and coughing. "Don't come near me, Alf," he said. "I think I've got a hefty dose of whatever the rest of the village has." I had to admit he looked pale.

"What are you doing outside?" I asked. "Get in and go to bed with a …" I was about to mention to my hot lemon and whisky remedy again when Claudia's face came to mind. "Hot water bottle," I finished instead.

"I'm no good at being ill," Mr Bramble insisted. "I can't sit still. I have to be doing something."

"I know what you mean. But you'll make yourself feel even worse. Promise me you'll go indoors and watch a film or something instead?" I wagged my finger at him. "I'd hate to hear you'd collapsed or become proper poorly."

"You're as bad as my wife." Mr Bramble laughed, and then when he started to cough, I pointed my finger at his front door and he gave me a salute and disappeared inside.

I continued my journey, passing the café, and noticing a poster on the door as I strolled past. Written in a hasty scrawl, it announced that the café was closed until further notice due to staff illness. In Whittle Stores, Rhona looked equally as pale as Mr Bramble, and admitted to feeling under the weather, but she was coping. Stan was tucked up safely in bed with a high temperature, but she was hopeful he would be better soon.

"Everyone in the village, well virtually everyone, has whatever it is. Dr Cooper from the surgery popped in for some milk earlier, and he said they've been inundated. He was making house calls until gone ten last night."

"Wow," I marvelled, thinking of Thaddeus. He was long past house calls.

"It's unheard of," Rhona reiterated, perhaps hearing a lack of commitment in my tone.

"Is there anything I can do for you?" I asked. "Deliveries or anything?"

"No, not at the moment, my flower. Thanks for the offer. Millicent is kindly doing a little of that. She never gets sick, and the bonus is, she can drive too."

"I'm learning," I said. It was true. I'd been having lessons for a while and had my test booked for the new year.

"Well next time then." Rhona smiled.

I nodded. "Just let me know if I can do anything for you at all. You know I will."

"You've such a kind heart, Alf," Rhona said as she waved me off, and I felt better than I had all day.

My newfound positivity didn't last very long, however. As I walked past Bob Gretchen's cottage, the door opened, and Grace strode purposefully up the drive to confront me, a child of around 8 years of age, following at her heels.

"I was hoping I'd see you." She didn't intend to stand on ceremony, clearly.

"Good morning, Grace," I tried to start in a friendly note, but this only served to feed the fuel of her fury.

"It's all your fault that the town is sick, and me and some of the other villagers, we want to know what you're going to do about it."

"My fault?" I stood still as this angry woman railed at me, completely in my face. I couldn't have been more perplexed.

"You've got strangers at the inn. People from somewhere foreign. Eastern Europe or somewhere. We've all noticed they only come out at night."

My stomach turned somersaults and I stared at Grace in horror. "What do you mean?" I managed to stammer.

Grace repeated what she'd said as though I was a complete imbecile. "Those new folks you've got staying at your inn? All dodgy accents and slicked back hair. Like vampires they are."

"You've seen them?"

"We've *all* seen them," she roared, her face contorted with fury. "They've been down here every night. Disturbing my kids. Disturbing everyone in the village."

I swallowed. I'd told Melchior none of his party could bother the villagers. This is how much respect he had for me. Quietly furious, I tried to turn my professional side to the fore in order to pacify Grace.

"I am so incredibly sorry about that, Grace," I began. "I'll have words with them. Try and ensure they don't come down here again."

"I'll be complaining to the council." Grace spat

at me. "We all will. There's plenty of us who have had enough of the goings-on at your inn."

"I promise I'll sort it out so there's no repeat of this. You're right of course. The villagers should not be bothered by this kind of thing."

Grace began another tirade. I held my hands up in mock surrender. "I really need to get back so that I can attend to this. Please excuse me," I begged and walked backwards.

"Nobody was sick till they came. You should make sure they've had all their inoculations before they stay at your inn," she shrieked after me.

I stumbled up the road, shaking in exasperation from the encounter, not entirely sure I'd managed it particularly well. My mind raced, trying to unpick all the things Grace had been saying. Of course she had put her finger on it. My guests *were* vampires, even if she only thought they were *like* vampires. Her indignance and fury came from a place of deep-rooted ignorance and innate prejudice about outsiders. If she knew them, maybe she would learn to like them.

But I knew them, and I have to say I wasn't feeling overly fond of them myself.

And the one thought that really stuck out was

her parting shot. "Nobody was sick before they came."

She was right about that.

I'd walked halfway up Whittle Lane, midway between the village and the turning for Whittle Inn. Now I turned and peered back down the road. I could make out the row of cottages, but it looked as though Grace had disappeared inside her home.

I slipped back the way I had come and took refuge in Millicent's doorway, trying to shrink into the wood while I waited for Millicent to answer my soft tap. It took an age for her to come to the door, and when she did she was clutching Sunny to her chest. Casting a final worried glance towards Dandelion Cottage, I threw myself inside.

Before my batty friend could say anything, I turned beseeching eyes on her. "Sorry to barge in, Millicent. I've not been entirely straight with you. But now I need your help."

"I knew something was going on with you." Millicent frowned. "You should have just turned them down when they asked to hire the inn as a venue."

"I know that now," I grumbled. "I didn't put two

and two together until it was too late. In fact it was grandmama who set me straight."

Millicent sniffed. "I'm not surprised. What does she think of all that's been going on?"

I shook my head sorrowfully. "You know, I haven't seen her in days. She's staying away. And Mr Hoo too. I've been really worried about him."

"More worried about the owl than Gwyn?"

I looked at Millicent and flapped my hands in exasperation. "Gwyn is dead, Millicent. She'll be perfectly alright. She's just sulking somewhere."

"She has every right to sulk. I'd sulk too," Millicent announced, looking peevish. I slunk forward in my seat, perfectly miserable, and Jasper licked my face.

"What am I going to do, Millicent?" I asked desperately. "Okay, I made a mistake allowing the vampires to stay at Whittle Inn. I'm a bit of a novice when it comes to the fanged ones. I'd never had much to do with them. My mother hated them."

"Your father isn't around?"

"No, I assume he's off doing top secret Circle of Querkus things." I sat back up, much to Jasper's disappointment. He obviously thought I'd been neglecting my personal hygiene, and he was doing a grand job of making me clean. "Do you think the vampires may be to blame for this mystery illness that's going around the village?" I tried to fend Jasper off, secretly enjoying his attention. Sunny sat on Millicent's lap watching us with interest.

"Oh, hmm." Millicent stared at me, busily thinking. I watched her as her mind scrolled through the people she knew who were ill. It took some time as there were lots of them. "Perhaps."

I groaned.

"Alf, you're so melodramatic," Millicent said matter-of-factly. "We have a small problem. We will solve it."

"We?" I asked, hopeful that she meant what she said.

"Of course, we. We're witches. We're not going to let a few pointy-toothed monsters get the better of us or our village." She placed Sunny carefully on the ground and stood. "I hope you're feeling strong. I need you to help me carry some boxes up to Whittle Inn."

In the end we borrowed Stan's van and carted four demi-johns of recently pressed blackberry juice, a dozen jars of locally produced honey, and dozens of small glass bottles up to the inn, along with numerous bags of what looked like vegetables. Millicent parked out the back of the inn, and I led her directly through to the kitchen to introduce her to Monsieur Emietter.

"Hello," she greeted the chef cheerfully. "We're going to need to borrow one of your largest pans and take up a little of your worktop space. I hope you don't mind."

"He doesn't speak English—" I tried to explain, but once Millicent got going, she was like a bulldozer. She waved away my explanations, ignored Monsieur Emietter's protestations, and started rooting through the cupboards looking for a large enough pan. We found one in the store cupboard. You could probably have fitted a small child into it.

Millicent dragged it out and carried it to the hob. "In the good old days the chef here used to keep a cauldron, you know."

"Really?" I asked. "If that's the case, it's probably upstairs in the attic. I don't think anything has ever been thrown away in the entire existence of Whittle Inn."

Charity picked that moment to join us. "Once you enter, you can't leave." I was sad to see her pale-face and red-eyes, she'd obviously been crying. I rushed over to give her a hug and she smiled, putting a brave face on things. "I'm okay, don't worry."

"That won't be the case for these vampires, I promise," I said. "They will most definitely be leaving. We'll get this wedding out of the way and then they're gone. Okay?"

Charity nodded. "Thirty-three hours."

"That's the spirit." I slapped the kitchen table. Monsieur Emietter looked across at me and said something I didn't comprehend. "I'm sorry." I shrugged in what I assumed was an overly-dramatic and gallic way that he would understand. "We need to do this." I indicated Millicent who had lit the stove and was now pouring the blackberry juice into the pot.

"Is there anything you want us to do?" Charity asked, and Millicent nodded.

"Run into the bar and fetch me your best bottle of whisky, Charity."

Charity balked at the job, and I knew why. "It's fine," I said. "Florence has cleared everything up. You won't know he was there." Charity swallowed and disappeared.

Millicent looked at me thoughtfully. "Is Florence around?" she asked, and I called my housekeeper.

She apparated almost immediately, a feather duster in her hand.

"Florence?" Millicent asked. "What did you do with the mess that was the vampire?"

"From this morning, you mean, miss? All that dust… and stuff?"

"Yes, all that dust and stuff."

"I've emptied it into the bin out the back, near the shed."

Millicent nodded happily and picked up a small glass bowl. "Be a darling. Rush back out there and scoop me up a handful."

Florence pulled a face. "Ewww."

"I can do it if you like?" I offered but Florence shook her head.

"No, no, miss. I'll go."

"Good stuff," Millicent said. "And while you're out find me a large splinter from the wood pile. About yay length." She held her hands about eight inches apart. Florence scooted away.

Millicent upended the brown bags of vegetables she'd brought along. Dozens and dozens of bulbs of garlic.

"Wow," I said and Monsieur Emietter came over to examine the garlic.

"*Ah délicieux!*" he exclaimed.

"Can you crush this for me, Monsieur Emietter?" Millicent asked and made a chopping notion. "*Écraser?*"

The spirit chef glanced at me warily. I'd insisted that all the food prepared at the inn while the vampires were staying should be garlic free. I nodded encouragement and his face lit up.

"*Enfin, je peux créer quelque chose de savoureux.*" The chef grinned.

"What did he say?" I asked.

Millicent widened her eyes. "I'm not sure. Something about at last … and savoury? Tasty?"

He set to with a large sharp knife, peeling the bulbs and individual cloves swiftly and efficiently before chopping each clove into ultra-fine slices, crushing them and then chopping them once more. The aroma of garlic filled the kitchen and made my eyes water a little.

"Phew, that stinks. We're going to have to give the kitchen a thorough clean before Sabien and his party awake."

"Let's worry about that later," Millicent urged. Charity was back with the whisky. Millicent cracked the lid of the pan and poured it into the mixture, the heat up high, then stirred in the honey and the garlic before re-fitting the lid tightly and smiling at the chef.

"Any chance of some lunch?" she asked.

Millicent kept the heat high for the next few hours and reduced the liquid, stirring intermittently. Interestingly, you could hardly smell the garlic at all. The combination of honey and blackberry meant the overwhelming scent was sweet and fruity. Monsieur Emietter popped the lid off the pot every now and again to examine the contents of the pan and sniff the steam. He seemed oddly taken with Millicent.

Millicent meanwhile kept a careful eye on the time. Eventually she looked around at Charity and me.

"Ladies," she said gravely. "This part of the cooking is done, now we need to turn it into something entirely more potent. We need to cast a spell."

"Oh I can't do that," Charity started to protest, backing away.

Millicent harrumphed. "Of course you can."

"I'm no witch," Charity insisted. "No offence, like."

"All women are witches. It's in our DNA," Millicent insisted. "Now Charity, come here."

Charity rolled her eyes and I smiled encouragement. "Is that true?" Charity asked, "that we're all witches?" I pulled a non-committal face.

"Of course it is," Millicent said, shooting me a look. "Come stand next to me here, Charity. That's it." Charity slipped in between Millicent and I, while Millicent removed the lid of the rapidly bubbling pot. "Now I need you to hold your hands out above the pan. That's right. Just there. And close your eyes." Charity did as she was told.

Millicent nodded at me and I leaned closer and held my hands above the pot too. "You can repeat my words, or you can say them in your head, Charity. But please follow the intent and the meaning and try not to think about what you're having for dinner this evening instead." Millicent sniggered. "Seriously now ladies. Let's do this." She stirred the thickening liquid. "Empty your mind, Charity."

I breathed deeply, noisily, so that Charity would hear my breath sounds and she joined me, breathing equally deeply into her diaphragm.

Millicent rasped in a low voice, "I call upon Hecate, upon the protector of witches, divine force, mother of mine. Hear our cry and grant us our desire."

I took the incantation up. "Protect those who habitually inhabit this inn, and those who live with us and among us in the village of Whittlecombe. Those for us and against us. Know no distinction." Millicent stirred the mixture, while I finished, "And grant us the strength to know our foes and to fend them off."

Millicent stepped back to pick up the bowl of Thaddeus's ashes and sprinkled them into the mixture. Now I stirred the gloopy mix, hard and fast. "With this potion, we ask that you heal the sick and support the weak," continued Millicent.

"Heal the sick and support the weak," I repeated and was delighted when Charity did the same.

Finally Millicent picked up the splinter of wood Florence had found and dropped it into the potion. "In Hecate's name, may this potion protect. So will it be."

"In Hecate's name, so will it be," I urged.

"So will it be," repeated Charity.

The spell complete, I allowed the hyper-energy rushing around my body to drain to my feet and bowed my head, grounding myself once more, and standing calmly. Beside me Charity followed my lead to the best of her ability. She had done well. "The things you get me into," she said.

Millicent turned the heat off from under the pan and smiled at us both.

"Well done. It's after three. We need to get cracking."

With the help of Florence and Monsieur Emietter, we decanted the potion into the small glass bottles and boxed them up. When we were finished there was a mug's worth left. Millicent made Charity and I drink half each. "We can't have you two getting sick, or coming under the vampire's spell, can we?" she asked, and I had to agree.

"Now time is of the essence," Millicent continued as we loaded Stan's van up with the bottles. "I need to dispense these among the villagers."

"Do you think they'll all drink the potion?" I asked doubtfully. My run-ins with some of the villagers of late, had me wondering whether they would trust anything linked to Whittle Inn.

"I don't know to be honest, Alf. I can but try. They have two choices, don't they? Drink it and be well. Don't drink it and possibly be ill. It can't hurt them. I mean look at you two, you both look better than you have for days."

I peered at Charity and she at me. I had to agree she looked less tired and pale.

"I'm going to need Charity's help, Alf. Can you cope till I drop her back?"

"Of course," I said, glancing at the horizon. The sun was starting to drop. There was probably an hour of light left. I wasn't looking forward to this evening at all.

It was Charity's turn to offer support. "Twenty-nine hours," she said. "Then it will all be over."

CHAPTER SIXTEEN

The vampires began drifting up from the cellar at around 7 p.m.

I waited for Sabien to put in an appearance and pulled him to one side. "I have terrible news," I said, and without further ado told him about the dreadful event of the morning. He listened carefully to what I said, a look of horror passing across his face.

"Where did this happen?" he demanded.

"Right here in the bar," I told him quietly, leading him to where the armchair had been positioned facing the window. "Thaddeus was seated here. Tied to the chair. We couldn't see him in the dark."

"You destroyed him?" Sabien asked mournfully.

The hackles on my neck bristled. *How dare he?* "Now stop there," I snapped, quivering with indignation. "The person you need to blame for this is whomever tied Thaddeus to that chair and sabotaged the electricity downstairs. We can't be held responsible for what happened. Yes, we opened the shutters, but no, we had absolutely no intention of hurting one of our guests."

My raised voice caused some curious looks from the other vampires gathering in the bar, no doubt to wage more destruction on my inn. I'd had enough.

"To a witch," I said pointedly, "*intent* is everything."

Sabien nodded curtly at this. "But even so, it was careless—"

"Opening the shutters was an *accident* Sabien. We couldn't have known." Fury bubbled inside me, like a champagne bottle that had been shaken too hard, desperate to explode. "Who destroyed Thaddeus?" I asked.

Sabien shrugged.

"He had a run-in with Gorkha just last night."

"I'm sure zat was something and nothing," Sabien said. "A disagreement about a woman, that's all."

"So Gorkha didn't do this?" I indicated the chair.

"No." He reconsidered and then offered. "Perhaps you are right, and ze whole thing was an accident."

Thaddeus had been tied to the chair. That hadn't been accidental. Sabien fixed me with his cool inscrutable gaze. He didn't want to discuss the incident further, that much was clear.

I changed the subject. "Talking of accidents, there have been many of those in the past few days. Your party are responsible for wrecking my furnishings and creating a terrible mess."

Sabien tried to cut me off, but I wanted to have my say. "I had an understanding with your son that none of your party would go into the village and bother the locals."

Sabien began to protest and I held my hand up. "But residents have reported back to me. You've been seen, and I am not happy. Not happy at all. We had a deal. You have broken your side of that."

"If it's a question of ze money—"

"When it comes to this inn and the village of Whittlecombe, it is about more than money. I believe you have all outstayed your welcome." I stood solidly in the centre of the inn and gazed around at the hushed wedding party.

From outside came the unmistakable sound of horses on gravel. I turned my head to the door.

"You can't make us leave, there are more guests

arriving now," Melchior said triumphantly, sidling up to his father.

Furious, I rounded on him. "This is my inn! I say who stays here and who doesn't. As far as I'm concerned the inn is closed." I turned on my heel and stormed back to the bar, ready to extinguish the lights and turn off the pumps. I'd put an end to this wedding once and for all.

Melchior and Sabien huddled together wondering what to do, but assistance for their plight came from an unexpected source.

"Please, Alf?" The clipped Russian accent that belonged to Kat. "Won't you reconsider?"

I turned to look at her. I wanted to ask her what she was playing at. Why was she marrying into this monstrous clan? But the look on her face held me back.

"You've worked so hard to stage this event, and everything is almost ready. This time tomorrow it will nearly be over. If you send us all away now, where will I get married? Who will help me the way you have? Please let us stay, Alf?"

What could I do? Kat looked at me with such beseeching eyes, I was a sucker, even though I thought she was about to make the biggest mistake of her life. Resisting the urge to smack my head against the bar's wooden surface, I had to reluctantly give in.

"Okay," I said. There was a whoop from some of the vampires, but I moved back into the general bar area, standing among the stools and chairs and tables, as the first plates began to float out from the kitchen, served by my friendly ghosts.

I stomped over to Sabien's table and glared at Melchior. "Nobody is to go down to the village tonight," I said. "If I hear that anyone has, you will pack your bags and leave. If I find out tomorrow, while you're sleeping during the day, that you broke this promise, I'll drag your coffins out of the cellar myself and have them opened on the lawn."

Melchior snarled at me.

"I want your word!" I slammed my hand down on the table and Melchior jumped.

Sabien lay his hand down on top of mine.

"You 'ave it," he said calmly. "Nobody will venture into ze village."

Charity arrived back from the village an hour or so later and was surprised to see how subdued the wedding party were. Gone was the hollering and disorderly behaviour of the previous few nights, instead the vampires conducted themselves like ladies and gentlemen, drinking in moderation and playing cards in some cases, or simply conversing among themselves.

"Alf had words," Zephaniah told her, stifling a grin, as he cleaned out one of the pumps for me.

Charity ogled me. "Did you?"

"I'd had enough," I said crossly. "They're pretty much taking my inn apart and making our lives a misery. I don't want that."

I offered Charity a drink, but she settled for a coffee. And why not? We had another long night ahead of us.

"How were the villagers?" I asked.

"Well." Charity twisted her face. "I don't know what's got into people down there. Lots of moaning about what's happening up here. I'd be surprised if they don't turn up here at midnight clutching pitchforks like they used to in the old days and set fire to the place."

"What?" I shrieked. "Don't say that!"

"Don't worry." Charity indicated the vampires. "They'd be on our side."

"What went on?" I asked.

Charity sighed. "For the most part the villagers

accepted Millicent's potion and said they'd take it. She's very persuasive, our Millicent."

I wondered if she had used magick. That would work on most of the villagers, I was sure.

"Then there were a few that refused point blank. Claimed you were in league with the devil and you needed to go back where you came from, that kind of thing."

I rolled my eyes. "Go back to where I came from? I only come from the next county. My father was born in this inn. So was my grandfather. What is wrong with people?"

"There's no accounting for stupid, Alf, you know that."

I did.

We had another half dozen guests show up through the course of the evening, but none of them were for Kat's side of the family.

"No friends, no family," I observed to Marc when he came up to the bar to hang out with me for a while. "It's a very one-sided affair."

Marc nodded, looking a little shifty, not meeting

my eyes. "What is it?" I asked. "You know something."

He cast a glance warily around, making sure Melchior and Sabien were otherwise engaged. I took that as a cue that we needed some privacy.

I walked to the frosted glass door, "Marc," I called, loud enough for any eavesdroppers to hear, "can I show you the cake? I could do with a second opinion." I shot Charity a meaningful glance, indicating that she should stop anyone following us, and then led Marc through to the kitchen. I firmly closed the door behind us, and switched on the light over the stove, startling Florence who was snoozing on a chair in front of me, waiting for orders from the bar. Of Monsieur Emietter there was no sign. Perhaps he was keeping Gwyn company somewhere.

"Sorry, Florence," I said, and she scuttled away into the storeroom.

Keeping my voice low, and an eye on the door to the passage, I addressed Marc. "What aren't you telling me?"

Marc reached into the back pocket of his jeans. He was always so understated in comparison to the other vampires who wore designer labels and the most expensive clothes they could find, and drowned themselves in cologne. Marc pretty much settled for jeans and casual t-shirts and shirts and sweaters, more relaxed about the world generally, and nicer for it.

He pulled out a sheath of envelopes and lay them on the counter. They were addressed to homes in Russia.

I shuffled through them. "Are these what I think they are?"

"Invitations to the wedding," Marc confirmed. "Kat wrote these and gave them to Melchior to send. He told me to destroy them."

"Does Kat think her family are coming?" I asked, disturbed once more by Melchior's deviousness.

Marc laughed without humour. "I doubt it. I think she knows him better than that."

I pushed a hand through my tangle of hair, getting my fingers snarled up in the knots. "I don't get it," I said. "Why is she putting herself through this. She's a beautiful young woman. She could do whatever she wants. Choose from so many different partners. What does she see in him?"

"Who wouldn't want immortality?" Marc asked. "Perhaps that's all there is to it. That and the fact that Melchior—or Sabien at least—are wealthier than most of us could ever imagine."

"Do you think that matters to Kat, though?" I

was puzzled. "The way she spoke about her mum to me the other day, I think she knows there's more to life than money and power."

"But that's what she gets by marrying Melchior," Marc said and although his tone was mild, I sensed an undercurrent.

"What is your relationship with Melchior?" I asked the question that had been burning in me since I'd first met him.

"Best mate. Best man." Matter of fact.

I studied Marc's face looking for clues, and he wriggled under my scrutiny. "Come on," I urged.

"He's always been there for me. Since I was turned."

"He didn't '*turn*' you?" I asked, unsure about the terminology.

"No, that was one of Sabien's wives."

"One of them? How many does he have?"

Marc shrugged. "I don't know. Lots."

"So, Sabien's wife turned you and Melchior became your... brother... by extrapolation, I suppose?"

Marc nodded. "That kind of sums it up." He tipped his head back, thinking. "It was over thirty years ago now, relatively recent in vampire terms, but it was a shock for me. Getting used to it. Particularly as I'm vegetarian."

"How do you cope?"

"I use a protein supplement. It's not ideal, but it works."

"Okay. And Melchior?"

"Showed me the ropes. Stuck up for me when the other vampires wanted to tear my throat out. That kind of thing."

"So you owe him?" Marc nodded. "But you definitely don't agree with him on everything." I remembered his reaction to the dress.

Marc shook his head. He flicked through the invitations again, then held them up. "I hate this. It's wrong. The way he treats her… the dress he had made for her… it's all wrong. He's trying to turn her into some sort of vampire queen. That isn't who she is. At all."

A noise from the passage startled us both. We looked over and waited, but the door remained closed and I couldn't sense anyone out there. Perhaps someone had just entered or exited The Snug or The Nook.

"You know what I think would be nice?" I whispered to Marc, and he turned his soft blue eyes on me. "If we could find a way to get Kat's mum here at the ceremony tomorrow. A bride deserves to be happy on her wedding day, and I have a feeling that seeing her Mum would make Kat the happiest woman in the whole of the south west of England."

"I'm sure it would," Marc replied, and I tipped my head pointedly at him.

CHAPTER SEVENTEEN

"It's raining!" My first thought on waking the following morning. After months of largely dry weather, it seemed ironic that today of all days, we would have rain. And heavy by the sound of it.

I closed my eyes and lulled by the rhythmic drumming of the cascade outside, quickly drifted away once more. My second thought jolted me wide awake: *wedding minus fourteen hours*! So much to do.

I'd set the alarm for ten, and now it began blaring beside me. I'd managed another magnificent four hours sleep, but today at least I could console myself with the knowledge that by the following morning it would all be over.

"I wonder where they'll honeymoon?" I said to no-one in particular as I swung myself out of bed. I tapped the bedframe where Mr Hoo liked to perch.

"Miss you, fella," I said and dragged my sorry self into the shower.

Thirty minutes later I was sharing tea, toast and marmalade with Charity. "We'd better ask Zephaniah to erect the marquee," I said.

"The forecast says it will pass over later this afternoon, early evening," Charity replied, showing me a weather tracking app on her phone. We put our heads together to watch a huge dense cloud pass over the whole of the south west of England.

"Why is that triangle red?" I asked, and Charity looked at the symbol more closely.

"It's a red alert. Danger to life. Risk of flash flooding," she said.

"Great." I picked up another slice of toast. "Have the marquee put up - just in case."

My own mobile rang, and Millicent's name appeared on the screen. I picked it up and accepted her call, smiling.

"Morning Mill—"

"You have to come down here, Alf," Millicent said, and there was alarm in her voice.

"Wha—"

"There's a meeting at The Hay Loft this morning to complain about the goings on at Whittle Inn. They're putting a petition together or something."

"At The Hay Loft?" I repeated. That blasted Lyle Cavendish and his interfering friend Gladstone Talbot-Lloyd no doubt. They'd been out to get me since I'd first moved to Whittlecombe. "Today of all days? The day the inn opens?"

"When better?" Millicent asked crisply. "Get down here. Fast."

I jumped to my feet, scattering toast crumbs across the table. "I have to go."

"What's the matter? Who was that?" Charity called as I dashed away, but I didn't stop to answer.

Damage limitation was all I could think of.

I ran through the rain into the village, barely noticing the fresh herby smell of the leaves as the hard rain bruised them, and the scent of damp earth rising from the ground. I was wheezing with exertion by the time I reached The Hay Loft. Bursting into the lounge bar, I found myself face to face with an angry mob.

At least, that's how it felt.

But rocking back on my heels and taking time to survey the room gave me a better sense of perspective.

Fortunately the 'mob' was much smaller than I'd imagined on my way into the village, and Millicent was already in situ, so I had at least one friend on hand. Some people were sitting on chairs, listening intently to the speaker, but appeared more bewildered and confused about the proceedings than anything else. There was a small minority gathered at the front, including both Grace and Bob Gretchen, who looked hostile, and seemed to be cheerleading the speaker on.

The speaker? I'd been right. None other than my old adversary Gladstone Talbot-Lloyd.

"What a surprise," I hissed under my breath. Soon after I'd moved into Whittle Inn, Gladstone had been implicated in his involvement with The Mori. He was a property developer who had wanted to buy the land Whittle Inn stood on, along with Speckled Wood. I knew Wizard Shadowmender and Mr Kephisto were looking closely at the awful man's past but given that he was a mere mortal—albeit one of the most annoying ones I had ever met—there was little they could do. So far Talbot-Lloyd remained at large and able to torment me.

I wondered whether I should confront him straight away, but I recognised there were people in the room who might rush to his defence if I did that, who might otherwise take a more balanced view. No. Far better to remain polite and measured, behave with dignity, and refuse to add fuel to the fire.

I smiled politely, at Talbot-Lloyd. "My apologies for intruding," I said, as the gathered congregation turned to look at me. I took a seat behind everyone else and folded my hands in my lap, planting my feet flat on the floor, grounding myself against the wave of indignant emotions that rushed through me. *'Calm and strength,'* I told myself. *'Calm and strength.'*

"Ah, Ms Daemonne," Talbot-Lloyd greeted me. Outwardly pleasant, but with eyes as cold as ice. "Delighted you could join us. We were just discussing some problems with your inn. Perhaps you could address the village's concerns?"

My invitation must have been lost in the post, I thought surveying the room once more. Out of the two-hundred and fifty or so folks who lived in Whittlecombe there were less than thirty present. "I'm happy to hear you out," I said, and smiled around the room once more, placing my hands carefully in my lap and maintaining a non-defensive body posture.

For some reason this infuriated Grace Gretchen, who launched straight into an attack. "Look at her sitting there like butter wouldn't melt in her mouth," she shouted, almost as though I couldn't hear what she was saying, and peering around at everyone else for support. "We all know that it's her fault that everyone in the village has been sick these past few days. Why else would she have sent around her lapdogs to hand out some potion to everyone."

Millicent's face went red and she shot up from her seat. I was sitting too far away to stop her.

"For shame, Grace," Millicent said. "I created that tincture to help relieve people's flu symptoms– and from my own pressed blackberry juice. The pharmacy at the health centre, and Whittle Stores, have been overrun and people haven't been able to find any relief. I was trying to help the community I love, and Alf was good enough to assist me by lending me her kitchen at Whittle Inn."

Grace started to retort, but Millicent rounded on her. "I've known you since you were hours old, Grace Gretchen. I baby-sat you when your own mother was poorly. We've been neighbours your whole life, but you would call me a lap dog to my face? What has become of you? For shame, Grace, for shame."

There were murmurs among some of the others gathered in the room. People cast side-long glances at me, others nodded at Millicent's words. Thanks goodness she was here. She had a long and excellent standing in the village.

Talbot-Lloyd interrupted. "Surely the point is that there are untoward goings on in Whittle Inn currently. Guests roaming the village at night, carousing and making a nuisance of themselves."

"Foreigners!" shrieked Grace and Millicent glared at her.

"Not forgetting rumours of witchcraft..." Lyle, the landlord of The Hay Loft piped up, and turned to me with a smug look.

Well that's no secret, surely? Hadn't my family always been witches. How had the villagers conveniently forgotten this?

"Ever since Ms Daemonne turned up, the village has suffered nothing but bad luck," Talbot-Lloyd went on. "While it may suit her to have a long hot summer so that repairs can be carried out on that old wreck of a building up the lane, the farmers have been suffering with the lack of rain."

I raised my eyebrows. *They surely couldn't hold me responsible for the good weather? Especially on the day the heavens had finally opened.*

"That's right," Bob Gretchen said. "The woman is bad news. Tom Potter said the day after Alf spoke to him, he lost his job, and he hasn't worked since."

I felt like an extra from Arthur Miller's *The Crucible*. This was getting ridiculous. Yes, I was sorry for Tom Potter, but did they really think I'd cursed him or something? Why would I do that? I just wanted to open my inn. The revelations were increasingly preposterous, but it was clear from the audience reaction that some people were buying into the rumours, lies and slander.

"Whittle Inn should not be allowed to remain open," someone else cried.

"It needs closing down," Bob Gretchen chipped in. "We can't have witches and ghosts, and all kinds of monsters in this village, casting spells and concocting poisonous potions. Think of the children."

"Yes, think of the children." Grace's voice rang out, bordering on hysteria. "I have two sons under ten. What will become of them if we allow this to continue? The council must take action and close the inn down."

The next comment chilled me to the bone. It came from somewhere near the front of the hall, but the speaker remained in shadow and with his back to me, so I couldn't see his face. He spoke clearly, calmly, his words cutting through me with the sharpest of blades. "In the old days we burned witches at the stake or drowned them in the village pond. Perhaps we should return to the old ways."

Uproar.

People leapt to their feet. Bob and Grace in agreement, Lyle and Talbot-Lloyd trying to make themselves heard, one or two more reasonable and rational folk making an attempt to mitigate against the last speaker, and call the comment out of order. Other villagers took the opportunity to slink away, passing me on their way out the front door, but not glancing my way.

I stood too, trying to catch sight of the man who had spoken of persecuting me, by the same means so many of my ancestors had suffered. Trembling, partly with anger, and partly with fear, I tried to fight my way through the group in front of me, but was held back by jostling, angry people. In vain, I stood on tip toes and peered above their heads, but there was too much movement, and whomever the speaker had been, he had melted away.

Giving up, I exited the hall in disgust, and stood simmering in the rain, my red face turned up to the sky, allowing the water to cool my burning cheeks. Millicent burst out after me just a few seconds later and stood beside me zipping up her jacket and positioning an old sou-wester on her head.

Before I could say anything, she held up a conciliatory hand. "Ignore them, Alf. It's a small and ignorant minority."

"The things they said though…"

"Persecution?"

"Who was that? I tried to find him?"

Millicent shook her head. "I don't know. I didn't even notice he was there until he spoke."

"If they all feel the same way…"

"They don't!" Millicent snapped. "The problem is that this minority is particularly vocal. They shout louder than anyone else and it fools us into thinking they speak for everyone. They absolutely do not."

She softened her tone and smiled reassuringly at me. "There are plenty of people in the village who like you and are fond of the inn and want to see it succeed. Don't let the nay-sayers put you off. Alf. Keep on doing what you're doing."

I nodded, feeling calmer. "Alright." I took a deep breath. "What news about the levels of the so-called illness in the village?"

"Better I think. I heard this morning there were more children back at school, and people are feeling well again."

"So is the cause of the illness the flu, or is it my fanged guests?"

Millicent shrugged. "Perhaps we'll never know."

"No reports of any of my guests roaming the village last night?

"None that I've heard."

I breathed a sigh of relief. "That's one thing, at least. So does this improved health in the village correlate with Millicent's Magick Blackberry Potion?"

"Definitely." Millicent laughed. "Stop fretting, Alf. Go back to the inn now and get ready for your big night. I'll see you later."

I grimaced, wondering if anyone else from the village would show up with her. Monsieur Emietter was planning on staging a magnificent buffet, it would be a shame if it all went to waste.

"I really hope I get some other takers," I said.

"Everyone loves a party. The only thing that may put them off is the weather!" She held her palms out to catch the rain as it pelted against her hands.

"I have a marquee... but it is supposed to clear up if the weather forecast is accurate."

"Here's hoping."

Chapter Eighteen

I returned to the inn to be showered with flowers.

Black and red roses, dozens and dozens of them, lying in boxes, so fresh I could still see the morning dew beneath the cellophane coverings. Sabien had hired his own florist to arrange the flowers and she and her assistant set about with gusto, creating magnificent flower arrangements that stood as tall as me.

Meanwhile, Charity took a few boxes of each colour to use to decorate the arbour. "Do you think we should just move the arbour into the bar?" she asked but I shook my head.

"This rain will stop," I said. And I believed that. Some sixth sense told me it was true, and in any case I trusted the forecast.

"Only, think on," Charity said. "The lawn will

get muddy if everyone is walking back and forth on it. I'm worried it will turn into a quagmire."

"Don't worry. Let me find Zephaniah and Ned. They can create a raised walkway using planks as duckboards for now, and if you and anyone else who is going backwards and forwards can use that, we'll lay the red carpet Sabien insisted on later, when the ground has dried off a bit."

Charity nodded and set to her next task. I didn't envy her. She'd be soaked to the skin in no time outside.

The inn was full of delicious scents—at last Monsieur Emietter was able to roast meats and create pies and pastries, vol au vents and open sandwiches. Delicacies began to find their way out to the buffet tables, and increasingly there was less room for anyone to manoeuvre in. This was where the main advantage of working with a team of ghosts came in: they can work anywhere and at any time and they don't take up much room.

I concentrated on re-stocking the bar and making sure we had plenty of champagne and white wine chilling in the cool store, and red wine breathing behind the bar. I avoided the cellar at all costs.

Upstairs, Kat was being attended by another of Sabien's hires, a make-up artist. The woman, goth to her very core and absolutely dripping in piercings, had come armed with several cases of make-up and the goddess knows what else. I'd effectively been banned from Kat's room, but every now and then I sent an excitable Florence upstairs to take a secret peep through the door.

That's another advantage of having ghosts on tap.

"What did you see?" I asked Florence the second time she came down.

"Miss Kat is having her hair messed with, I think," she replied, looking puzzled.

"Messed with?"

"Covered in gloopy stuff."

"Like hair dye?"

"Yes, perhaps that's what it is."

"Aww," I said. "She has such glorious coloured hair. It's a shame to mess with it."

"I find it strange," Florence said wistfully. "We didn't do such things in my day. I think I would like to have had pink hair like Charity. But it's not natural, miss."

"No it's not but it's bit of fun, that's all," I laughed. Florence may have found it strange, but she also found it entrancing, and off she went again to sneak another look at Kat.

Just as the forecast—and my sixth sense—had told me, the rain stopped at four-ish, and it wasn't long before the sun came out again and the temperature started to rise. It would be dark within two hours, but at least now we could start the rest of the preparations for the wedding in earnest.

Charity had finished the arbour and it looked magnificent. Standing on the slightly raised stage, covered in red and black roses, and green hedera that had been woven in and out of the wooden frame, and hung with fairy lights, the setting was glorious and truly magickal. Zephaniah and Ned were now putting out dozens of chairs for the guests to sit on, and we'd hired a few fancy cast iron fire baskets to keep guests warm if the evening was chilly.

I had a table set up and Florence was covering this in red and black table cloths and setting out champagne flutes, all prepared for the first toast.

Practically everything was ready.

The sun sank into the trees to the west of us, my cue to ensure everything was ready for the vampires as they rose. Melchior had his bedroom upstairs where he would change into his suit and relax, probably with Sabien, Gorkha and Marc, before we all assembled in the garden just before midnight.

My own guests would be arriving at the inn at around half-seven for drinks and buffet and some—hopefully—wonderful music. Luppitt Smeatharpe and the Devonshire Fellows were already warming up in The Snug. It sounded a little like a chorus of feral felines caterwauling, but I could hope it would get better.

I walked the inn and grounds once more, armed with a clipboard and my checklist. Everything seemed to be in order. Full dark was less than ten minutes away. It was time for me to make myself look presentable.

At that moment my mobile began to ring. Then Charity's. Then the house phone.

Charity and I exchanged glances and reached for our phones. Rhona's name appeared on the screen of my mobile. My stomach lurched. I could only hope Stan hadn't taken a turn for the worst.

"Rhona?" I said.

"Alf. Thank goodness. We have a terrible situation. We need your help," she gabbled, breathless.

"What's the problem?" I asked, alarmed by the panic in her voice.

"All that rain—"

"Yes?"

"Where the soil has been so dry these last few months? It's crumbling away. There's been a landslip at Whittle Folly."

"Oh no!"

I knew the Folly. It was a flat circular area cut into the forest. The scouts and Whittlecombe youth club had buildings there, little more than flimsy huts. The car park was used as a base to walk in the surrounding forest.

"It's worse. The slide has taken down the scout hut and apparently there were a couple of kids in the building. They're trapped."

"The emergency services?"

"On their way, Alf. But we need as many people down here to help as we can now. Do you have any bodies you can spare?"

"We're on our way!"

"It's probably better if you stay here," I said to Charity. "In case guests start turning up. They won't all know about the emergency in the village. One of us should be here."

"What should I do?"

"Just keep them entertained. Feed them, serve them drinks and make merry." I ran to grab my jacket, Charity following at my heels.

"What about the wedding?" Charity looked worried.

"If I'm not back, just go ahead. "You'll do a great job!"

Turning about I looked for people to take to the Folly with me. At that moment Kat appeared on the stairs, wearing jeans and a t-shirt, with a towel around her shoulders. Her hair had been dyed black and the make-up artist had started applying base coat on her skin. "What's going on?" she asked.

"There's been a landslide in town and some children are trapped. No time to explain. I'm leaving Charity in charge. I need to get going. I'll be back soon." I waved and made for the door.

"I'll come!" she said.

"You can't do that. You have to get ready."

"This is more important," Kat insisted.

"It's your wedding!" Charity called, aghast,

But Kat was already climbing the stairs. "Let me just grab some boots."

"I can't wait, Kat."

"I'll be right behind you," Kat took the stairs two at a time and rushed back to her room.

I arrived at Whittle Folly, on the other side of the village, just as a fire engine drew up. There was a police car already in attendance and an ambulance too. I spotted George Gilchrist, dressed in a suit, speaking to one of the uniformed officers. He'd obviously been on his way to my party when the call came through. The fire officer joined them, and they huddled together for a conflab before splitting off.

Several families were here, standing together. Fathers ashen-faced, mothers crying. Primarily among them, Grace Gretchen, her hands clasped to her mouth. I joined Millicent and indicated Grace. Millicent nodded, grim-faced. "It's her boys in the hut. The cub scouts meeting this evening had been cancelled because the Akela is ill, but Grace's boys and a couple of others had broken in there to play."

Two boys managed to get out in time, but both of Grace's sons were still inside when the excessive and sudden rain we'd endured caused the landslide. Loose, wet mud swamped the hut and the building had collapsed. Both boys were still unaccounted for. I felt sorry for Grace and wished with all my will that the boys were safe in a pocket of space inside the rubble.

The fire officer began organising his crew while we all stood by waiting for instruction. There was a sense that everyone wanted to wade in and get started, but being very British about the whole thing, we thought it best not to jump in without someone official's say-so.

Time seemed to stretch interminably on, until the fire commander addressed us. We were to form a human chain along the side of the gully that stretched from the collapsed building to the road. His team would work at the building itself and hand items to the first in the chain and we were to pass them along and deposit them far from the site of the collapsed building. Specialist equipment had been sent for, but it would take time to arrive.

Slipping into the mud, a thick oozing river of slime, we lined up and the process began. Carefully the fire officers and the police pulled planks and boards away from the collapsed building, peeling back a layer of rubble, section by section. Each piece was passed down and added to a growing mound in the car park. Progress was slow but sure.

Some of the pieces were heavy and required two or three of us to manoeuvre them at once. We slipped and slid about, rapidly finding ourselves covered in mud from head to toe. I glanced up the line to see George, his shirt sleeves rolled up, looking like a particularly filthy coal miner. Further down the line, Kat, usually so pristine and elegant, pulled her weight with the best of them, and to my total surprise I spotted Marc with her. What I could see of his skin beneath the layer of muck, glowed eerily in the moonlight.

We worked solidly for twenty minutes, until the fire officer called a halt and asked us to remain quiet. We could hear the faint crying of a child among the ruins of the scout hut. I watched from a distance as the fire officers tried to get to the sound, but they and their equipment were too bulky. They shouted down to the boys and received a response. Grace screamed for her sons and tried to get through but was held back by Bob. "Don't get in the way," he told her, and she sagged in her father's arms, weeping and lamenting.

Another fire officer rushed to the engine to grab some rope and there was more toing and froing and I saw the police officer on his radio, but very little else seemed to happen.

I snuck up to George to see what was happening. Beneath the layers of dirt that caked his face I recognised his tension. "What's up?" I asked quietly.

"We've found the missing boys, but we can't get

to them. We've tried putting a rope down, but one of the boys seems to have broken his arm and the other won't leave without his brother. We need someone slimmer, but also with a long reach. Or we're going to have to wait for the specialist equipment to get here from Exeter."

"Tall and slim?" I repeated and glanced back down the line. "I think I may have the perfect solution. Not only that, but his vision in the dark is exemplary."

I made my way over to Marc, explained the situation, then, with both of us slipping and sliding, led him back to George. George quickly introduced him to the fire commander and they discussed whether Marc was up for a bit of rescue work. Of course Marc readily agreed. I knew he would. That was the sort of person he was.

Kat came to stand with me, and we watched as the fire officer strapped Marc into a harness. Lying on his front Marc shuffled towards the hole. Slowly and gently he edged into the confined space. One false move and all the rubble could tumble down and crush the boys beneath. Kat and I gripped each other's hands, and like the other onlookers we remained silent, every muscle and fibre straining in sympathy with Marc as he wriggled forwards. The very earth seemed to hold its breath. For a second I doubted even he was slender enough to work his way through but at last his head was inside and then his shoulders, and millimetre by millimetre he disappeared from view.

The wait seemed interminable. The fire commander at the edge of the hole, bent forwards, issuing gentle instructions. Finally we spotted a tug on the harness and the rescuers gently pulled on the rope. Marc inched out backwards, nice and slowly, clutching the older boy underneath his armpits. The boy's hand dangled slightly awkwardly, and I winced in empathy.

The child was taken from Marc and wrapped in a blanket by the waiting paramedic. Grace ran forwards, crying to hug her son, and the paramedic led them both towards the ambulance. Bob Gretchen took her place, his jaw tight, observing as Marc prepared to head back into the hole.

The going in this time was just as difficult as before. Marc took it slowly, painfully so, moving in meticulous and gentle increments, but this time at least the coming out was easier. A little boy of about eight, the one I'd previously seen with Grace, was taken from Marc's arms, crying for his Grandad and Bob reached out to him and held him tight.

We onlookers sighed in mutual relief, and Marc stood to remove the harness, just as the rest of the building collapsed. There were cries of horror as Marc slipped, Kat shrieked and held her hands to her face, and I grabbed her arm in fright. It looked as though he would be swallowed up by the building as it moved, shifting beneath his feet, more wet sludge pouring down from the hilltop to cover the rubble and crush the flimsy structure to smithereens.

But Marc was in safe hands. The fire officers at the other end of his harness, tightened their grip and yanked him back. He fell onto the ground, a relieved look on his face.

As one we began to applaud. Everyone crowded around both him and the rescue services, shaking hands and patting backs, gripping shoulders and hugging tightly. More villagers joined those who had been working at the Folly, rushed to thank the rescuers and congratulate them on a job well done. A fresh bout of cheering followed quickly, when it was announced that both boys would be absolutely fine. Nicholas, the older of the two, had a suspected fracture of his wrist, but the younger boy was simply shaken. They would both be taken to the hospital to be checked out.

We all milled around in the darkness, laughing

at our filthy appearances, and generally allowing the adrenaline to bubble up and subside. I couldn't help but notice how Kat looked at Marc, admiration in her eyes. Maybe tonight we all looked at him like that. It was a heroic deed. A good job, well done.

I smiled up at George as he stood beside me. "I'm so glad that turned out for the best," I said. "What a relief."

"Thanks to you and your friend," he said indicating Marc.

"Yes. Who'd have thought it? One of the very people some of the villagers have been railing against these past few days, and he came up trumps and saved Grace's son."

George frowned. "How do you mean?

"Oh ignore me," I said. "It's a long and complicated story, and it's wearing me out." I rubbed my forehead, my skin itched where the mud was drying. "I must look a right state." Everyone else did.

"You look beautiful to me," George said, and right there, in the mud, in the darkness, surrounded by four dozen people he leaned down and kissed me full on the lips. A soft kiss. A lingering kiss. The promise of so much more.

I gasped in surprise and George drew away, his

eyes shining. "I've wanted to do that for a long time." I giggled in delight, wishing he would do it again.

The rescue services were beginning to pack their equipment away. They would return at first light to investigate and secure the site, but for now they had done all they could. The villagers were starting to make a move too, and George pointed the time out to me. After nine.

"You have a wedding to host, don't you?" We both turned to Kat.

"We should go," I said to her. "Melchior will be waiting for us."

I saw an emotion pass across her face. Disgust? I couldn't be sure. But just as soon as I spotted it, it had gone again, and she had shut those feelings down. Without looking at Marc, she nodded at me. Time to go.

George indicated his car. "I'll drive us back up to the inn."

I nodded, but before I took my seat, I turned and called to those remaining at the Folly. "Hey, guys." People stopped chatting and turned to where I stood with George, Marc and Kat. Some of these same people had attended the meeting in the morning. A few of them had spat their hatred at me and the inn. One of them might well have called for witches to be burned at the stake once more. I didn't know who that had been, but I had to put it behind me for now. It was as Millicent had said, a small minority after all.

"Don't forget, it's the official opening of Whittle Inn tonight. There's food and champagne and music—and this lovely lady is getting married at midnight." I indicated Kat, standing alongside me. She may have blushed, but it was impossible to tell given the amount of dirt she was layered in. There were nudges and cat calls among the villagers. "It's going to be a blast, so please come along if you want to." I didn't wait for a reaction, unwilling to hear anyone say they wouldn't be seen dead in my inn, or were unwilling to fraternise with witches.

George twisted his face at the amount of muck we carried into his car, but there was nothing else for it. Showers and fresh clothes could be found at the inn.

George parked at the side of the inn, behind Jed's van. I looked away from it, not wanting to ruin the evening, and the lingering memory of George's kiss.

Instead, I linked arms with Kat and pulled her

along to the front of the inn and the main door, where we paused to take in the spectacle of the party. Coloured fairy lights were lit up on the lawn and around the arbour, the braziers were burning, and people were milling about with glasses of champagne, including—I was happy to see—guests from the village. I could hear the Devonshire Fellows playing their Elizabethan dances and I was ecstatic to note they were all in tune and in mighty fine voice. Mellow light streamed from the windows of the inn, lighting up squares of lawn, and people were coming and going through the front door.

Whittle Inn was alive and well and open for business, properly buzzing. It truly was a magical sight, and for once the tears in my eyes were tears of happiness.

Any feelings of contentment were dashed to smithereens as soon as we entered the inn however. Kat had been turning about, remarking about the pretty lights illuminating the stage, and the gorgeous flowers around the arbour, but as we stepped into the inn itself, we were pulled up short. Melchior waited for us in the centre of the lounge bar, his body taut with fury, flanked by Gorkha and another of his young friends

Before I could do or say anything, Melchior marched towards us and then reached out and grabbed Kat viciously by the upper arm, dragging her towards the fire.

"Where have you been?" he cried. "Look at the state of you!"

George following us in, rushed forwards. "Hey, hey! What do you think you're doing?" He tried to step in between Kat and Melchior. "Take it easy mate."

Melchior's head shot forwards, his lips curled and his fangs on show. George reeled backwards in shock, but still reached for Kat. Melchior rushed at George, pushing him out of the way as though he was swatting at a bothersome fly. Like all vampires, Melchior had immense strength. George flew backwards, collided with one of the large wing-backed armchairs and tumbled to the floor, winded.

I ran to help George. Around us, vampires hollered and laughed. Kat shrieked and tried to pull away, but Melchior shook her like a rag doll. "Have you no pride? You arrive here just hours before we're due to marry looking like some low-life tramp. You bring shame on me and on my family. If you can embarrass me so much on the biggest day of my life, how will you behave further down the line? I should have left you where I found you, in the gutter in Chernoistochinsk with your whore mother."

I heard an angry deep-throated roar and felt a rush of wind as a shadow blasted past me at great speed. I barely had time to turn my head, and there was Marc, his hands around Melchior's throat, his nails dangerously embedded in the skin, his own fangs unsheathed and his eyes red and wild.

"Enough," he hissed.

At once, there were vampires with hackles raised all around the room. Melchior's dark-haired vixens had their claws out, backs rounded like scalded cats, snarling and spitting like an angry fire. Gorkha paced, his breathing heavy, his arms tense by his sides and his hands rolled into fists. I was reminded of the confrontation between Thaddeus and Gorkha, and shivered at the memory of how that had turned out.

Melchior struggled for a second, then relaxed, gazing up at Marc with amusement. "How the worm turns." His eyes flashed black with malevolence.

"Why can't you behave with a modicum of common decency, Melchior? How difficult can it be?" Marc asked. "Your notion of how vampires behave is hopelessly outdated. This is the twenty-first century. You behave like a playboy and have no social conscience or moral compass."

Melchior rolled his eyes. "Save me from your sanctimonious drivel, Marc. You've never really fitted in as a vampire, have you? I don't know what my mother was thinking when she turned you. My father should have finished you off."

"Perhaps he should have done. The past few decades watching you torment innocent people and behave like a spoilt brat has completely soured me for a life of eternity, I can assure you." Marc shook Melchior one last time and opened his mouth as though he would tear the man's throat out.

"Marc," Kat said, reaching for him with tears in her eyes. She lay her hand on his arm. "Please don't."

"Why?" Marc asked, staring at Kat with complete bemusement. "Just give me one good reason."

Kat reached out to stroke Marc's face. "Why stoop as low as him?" she whispered, so quietly, only Melchior, George and I would have heard.

"If you despise him so, why are you marrying him?" Marc asked, his tone plaintive, his eyes beseeching, as though he would throw his arms around her and whisk her to safety. "Run! Run far away in the opposite direction. You can do so much better."

Melchior wriggled in Marc's more relaxed grip, almost free. "I've wanted Kat since I first clapped eyes on her. You know that. We made an agreement. If she marries me, I'll see to it that her family will be better off and live long, happy and blessed lives."

Marc tightened his grip once more, scowling into Melchior's amused face. "You've coerced her to marry you on the grounds that if she doesn't, you'll hurt her loved ones, haven't you? You've threatened them. That's no blessing. Not for Kat or her family. Melchior you never fail to stoop lower and lower. You're repulsive."

Kat reached for Marc's hands wrapped so tightly around Melchior's throat, and smoothed his taut knuckles with her soft fingers. "Let him go now. Please," she urged him.

Marc groaned like a wounded animal and didn't immediately release his quarry.

"Please," Kat repeated. "You just have to trust me." The look she gave the tall vampire would have melted glaciers. Marc sighed and slackened his grip. Melchior wiggled free, and instantly reared up into Marc's face. I gasped, certain it would all kick off properly now and Marc would come out of it worst off. I caught hold of George's arm, frightened of what I would see and unsure how to stop it.

"Enough!" Sabien's stern rebuke as he descended the stairs, brought order to the room. Vampires stood down, smoothing their ruffled feathers.

Like caged fighters Melchior and Marc stood back from each other, unable to break their gaze. Sabien stepped between them. "Time is rolling on. We have a wedding to attend to. Let's get on with it, shall we?"

"You have the strangest life," George marvelled, as he pulled on his freshly laundered and dried shirt. Florence had been busy sponging his suit clean, and washing, drying and ironing his shirt. My housekeeper was a marvel. We had both showered and were now getting ready in my own suite of rooms. It felt a little odd to have George here in my private quarters, but all the bedrooms were taken. I tried to keep my eyes firmly averted. "And you have the oddest friends."

I made a valiant effort not to look at George while he buttoned his shirt, but my cheeks may have been a little pink. I concentrated instead on trying to tame my tangle of freshly washed hair. If only there was a spell for eliminating frizz, I could set myself up and make my fortune by selling to similarly-afflicted women around the world.

"These vampires are not really my friends," I corrected him, while adding copious amounts of product, and combing it through with my fingers, trying to define the shape of the loose spirals. "Well, maybe with the exception of Marc. He seems a good sort. Sabien I wouldn't trust as far as I could throw him."

"And Melchior?"

I thought about it for a second, but I didn't need long. "He's a spoilt brat, as Marc said. A waste of space. But incredibly dangerous because of that. You need eyes in the back of your head where he's concerned. You really don't want to cross him."

"Hasn't it worried you? Having vampires to stay at the inn? What if they'd been off feeding among the local population?"

I swivelled on my stool to look at him. "Millicent and I took care of that." I wondered if there was any of Millicent's Magick Blackberry Potion left in the kitchen. I ought to dose George up while I was thinking of it.

George pulled his suit jacket on and inspected it

for stains or stray specks of mud. "Florence did a great job."

"Of course she did." Giving up on my hair, I watched him. He spoke about Florence so matter-of-factly, and yet eight weeks ago, he hadn't even believed in the existence of ghosts. Today it hadn't even crossed his mind to question whether the vampires were real.

"How did you feel when Melchior went for you?" I asked, curious as to his emotional state given this latest bunch of challenging creatures.

"Terrified." He grimaced. "If I hadn't seen it with my own eyes... You know, I'm beginning to think witches are pussycats in comparison."

I laughed. "Some are, some aren't."

He offered me a hand, and when I took it he pulled me from my stool, and held me close, his eyes smiling down into mine, his lips curled in amusement. "Which are you? Pussycat or lioness?"

"You'll have to find out."

A knock on the door interrupted us, and I tutted, closing my eyes in resignation. The joy of being constantly on call when you work in hospitality.

"Alf?" Charity's voice from the other side. "I need a hand. We have more guests arriving.

"Coming now," I called back and pulled away,

but George held me by the elbow for a second longer.

"I am going to find out," he promised, his voice low, sending shivers from my scalp to my toes.

I grinned and skipped out of the door to join Charity downstairs. "You're going to love this," she said, her eyes wide as I joined her.

'This' turned out to be a large convoy of guests arriving from the village, led by Millicent. Charity and I joined them out on the circle of drive in front of the inn. I recognised several faces from the meeting earlier in the day. Those that had been angry with me and had demanded the inn be closed.

"Hi," I said, slightly alarmed at finding this gathering outside the inn now, and hoping they weren't going to cause trouble.

One of the original ringleaders from the meeting stepped up. "Ms Daemonne, on behalf of the residents of Whittlecombe, we wanted to apologise for our behaviour recently. Your family has a long-standing reputation in the village, and Whittle Inn has always been highly thought of. We listened to certain personalities who were rumour-mongering and that was very wrong of us." He paused, cleared his throat and continued. "We want to show our appreciation to you for bringing some of your guests down to Whittle Folly this evening and for your part in the rescue of the children in the scout hut. We can't thank you enough and hope you won't hold our behaviour against us."

"Hear, hear," echoed others in the group.

Millicent nodded along with the chorus, looking as pleased as punch.

The spokesperson continued, "You have many friends in the village, Ms Daemonne, please don't imagine that's not the case."

I flushed with pleasure and beamed around at everyone. "You don't know how much it means to me to hear you say such things," I said. "I hope I'm always able to do my best for the village and play a part in the community's wellbeing. Now!" I gestured around at the tables, groaning under the weight of Monsieur Emietter's bounteous buffet. "Please make yourself at home. Eat, drink and make merry. We've a wedding at midnight!"

CHAPTER NINETEEN

At five minutes to midnight, with the full Hunter's moon high in the sky above Speckled Wood, and the fairy lights glittering all around us, guests from Whittlecombe village, vampires, ghosts, witches and all, took their places together in order to await Whittle Inn's first wedding.

Melchior dressed in top hat and tails, and flanked by Gorkha and Sabien, waited at the arbour with the celebrant Sabien had organised to officiate the vows. As a last-minute change of plan, Kat had asked George to step in and walk her down the aisle, because Marc, who had previously agreed to do so, now flatly refused to do so.

I stood in my place at the front, watching for Kat to arrive at the inn's door, so that I could give the

Devonshire Fellows the nod. At last I spotted her, so I nodded at the musicians. Robert Wait leapt straight in and the other fellows followed suit with a romantic wedding song, sweet and lilting. As one, the congregation turned to observe Kat and a communal gasp was released into the night air.

The make-up and hair artist had surpassed herself—there could be no denying. Kat was at once entrancing and magnificent, while simultaneously appearing cold, fearsome and terrible. Her red and black dress fitted to perfection and shimmered as the beads caught the light. Her normally lightly tanned skin had been powdered to a smooth translucent blue-white. Her face was sculpted with eyes at once smoky and yet piercingly sharp. Her lipstick was black to match the new colour of her hair, twisted into a complicated hairstyle.

As she drew closer to me, I glimpsed my first look at the ornate crown that Melchior had insisted she wore. Over a foot high, I imagined it was cruelly heavy. It had been crafted in gold and jewels, with spokes that ran off the head piece and cradled Kat's head, digging in around the jaw line and the back of the neck in five or six places. I could imagine it pinching as she tilted her head or altered her posture.

It spoke of Melchior's control and obsession, and Kat's submission and acquiescence.

I heard the gasps and murmurs in the congregation behind me, and hoped that having so recently built bridges with some of my nearest neighbours, this weird and oddly unsettling wedding wouldn't serve to burn them down again.

As George drew level with me, Kat dropped his arm. He helped her onto the stage—with some difficulty given the volume of the dress and the weight of the head dress—then joined me at the front. The Devonshire Fellows finished their song and the celebrant moved to the centre of the arbour and raised his hands.

"I welcome you all, friends and family of the bride and groom, and express my gratitude that you have chosen to join Melchior and Ekaterina on this, the most important night of their lives thus far," he intoned.

"This evening, in the presence of our lords, gods and goddesses, we will bear witness to the miraculous power of love, and join Melchior and Ekaterina in marriage. We will join their souls and unite them as one in their hearts."

I shuddered at the words. Tonight Kat's mortal

life would come to an end, and her immortal life must surely commence.

I glanced at George, wondering whether there was anything we could do to stop this madness, but he misconstrued my look and only smiled at me and took my hand. I turned to face forward again but noticed the lights of a car coming up the lane. A taxi. It was travelling quickly and as it sped along the drive it scattered gravel everywhere, causing many guests to swivel around to look. We were all wondering who could possibly be arriving this late in the ceremony.

The taxi drew up in front of the inn, and two women leapt out of the back and ran towards us. The front passenger seat also opened.

The celebrant raised his voice calling my attention away from the interruption. "Marriage is a conscious act of will that entwines two lives for eternity. Tonight, Melchior and Ekaterina will affirm and declare each other as partners in life and in death, and celebrate their union, and their immortal life's path together."

"Ekaterina!"

One of the women ran up the red carpet towards the dais shouting Kat's name. I stepped forward, thinking she meant to disrupt the service. "Ekaterina," she called again, a slim woman in her fifties with hair caught up in a scarf. She had the look of someone who had lived a hard life. There were bags underneath her eyes, and deep-set lines cut around her mouth, but still she appeared full of energy. She looked at me desperately as I reached to hold her back, took my hands, with her own that were dry and calloused, and began speaking in Russian.

At this, Kat turned slowly—for the horrendous crown only allowed for slow considered movements—and stared in disbelief.

"Mama?" she whispered.

"Yes, *Malyshka*!"

"Mama!" Kat screeched and wobbled across the dais towards her. Melchior snatched his hand for her to yank her back to her place, but Kat turned to him as he pulled, and with one well-placed right hook to his nose, landed him squarely on his backside.

I laughed in happy astonishment. I'd recognised a certain feistiness in Kat before, and to be fair she must have caught him off balance, but even so, I applauded her for taking out the bridegroom so spectacularly. He sprawled on the floor, clutching at his nose, blood leaking between his fingers, fury in his eyes, his mouth opening and closing in indignation. Fearing for Kat's safety I leapt on to the stage and shielded her from him as he tried to stand. She clutched at me as I helped her down the steps to the lawn where her mother enveloped her in a warm embrace. Sabien helped Melchior to stand but held him back.

They were joined by the second woman, and Ekaterina yelped with surprise. "Ludmilla," she cried, and the women hugged and rocked together, talking rapidly in Russian so that nobody else could understand a word. I looked around at the guests. The vampires were uneasy, wondering what was happening, but the locals were nodding and smiling and very much enjoying the spectacle. I suspected, this was one wedding they would be talking about for years to come.

"Mama, it was my dearest wish you should be here." She turned to the other woman, "Ludmilla," she asked in English. "How did you get here?"

Ludmilla looked around. "A phone call. Flight tickets," she replied in broken English. "All paid. All taxi."

Kat shook her head, confused, "But who? Who did that?" She looked at me. "Alf?"

I shook my head. "Not me, but ..." I looked

around, spotted Marc on the periphery and waved him over. "If I'm right...?"

Sabien's cultured French accent cut into the general hoo-ha. "Shall we continue? The moon eez high. We must complete ze ceremony."

Kat waved him away impatiently.

Melchior's cold voice behind us cut through once more. "Kat. It's past time. We must do this now."

Kat didn't even acknowledge him. "Marc?" she asked softly, and he walked forwards. She took his hands. "Thank you," she said. "You made my dream come true."

"You made me a promise, Ekaterina," Melchior insisted, his voice sounding thick, the growl ominous, his once-pristine white shirt soiled with blood was a promise of more violence to come. "We have an agreement."

And with that he turned. With a roar he reached for Kat once more, his eyes glittering with black death, mouth open and fangs unsheathed. His nails tore into the skin at Kat's shoulder and she shrieked in fear. He threw her towards Sabien and flew at Marc. There was pandemonium in front of the dais as the congregation scattered in panic, trying to put some distance between themselves and the flailing vampires.

Melchior had a tight hold of Marc and had forced him to his knees. Sabien gripped Kat's shoulders, his own nails, black talons of doom, his teeth shining—reflecting the light from the Hunter's Moon.

Kat's wail of despair at Marc's predicament turned into a scream of pain and she clutched at her head. The hideous headdress, so tightly clamped around her jaw, began to compress her skull. From my relatively close vantage point I could see how it gripped her cheeks and pinched the skin around her chin.

I rushed towards her, not knowing how I could help, but intent on freeing her if I could get close enough. If I could only wangle my fingers inside the gilded cage that held her prisoner and pull her free, or somehow loosen it enough to prevent her skull being crushed, but my subconscious knew that one targeted blow from Melchior or Sabien, or any of the other gathered vampires, could finish me off for good.

I hadn't even made it within two feet of Kat when a blinding flash drove me to the floor, arms raised to protect my head and face. I heard Kat shriek again, and Sabien squawk in fury. Tentatively uncovering my face, I looked up, and was startled to see Wizard Shadowmender standing on the dais, wand drawn, a look of fury on his face, the like of which I had never seen before.

With another sharp flick of his wand, the evil cage gripping Kat's head loosened. Orange energy, spun and coiled around the vampires, holding them locked in place. They could move their limbs, but not exit the cannily woven forcefield. Only Marc, squatting on the ground, rubbing at his neck, had his freedom.

Wizard Shadowmender reached down to help me up. "Really, Alf," he said, his tone mild, a slight curl at the edges of his mouth. "You do get yourself into such scrapes."

I laughed, a little shakily, and turned to Kat. "Are you alright?" I asked, breathless with the fear that had gripped me.

She nodded. "Thanks to this gentleman."

"This is Wizard Shadowmender," I introduced them to each other. "He always seems to be around when I really need him."

"Thank goodness." Tears of relief shone in Kat's eyes. She reached for me and clasped my hands in hers.

"I'm sorry," I said. "It was an error of judgement on my part. I should never have agreed to let this wedding go ahead."

She shook her head. "No. Don't be sorry. I do not believe it was your decision to make. They were holding my family hostage. And I would have done anything to ensure my mother and sister's safety." She smiled her thanks at Shadowmender, then turned her misty eyes back to me. "I have one more favour to ask of you. You made a potion," she said. "It protected the village."

"Yes." I wondered where she was going with this.

"You can make it again?"

I looked at Millicent who was standing in front of the dais, listening intently. She nodded.

"Yes," I said again.

Kat looked me directly in the eye, her face grave. "Alf. Can I entrust you with the protection of my beloved mother and sister?"

Now I was beginning to understand. I glanced at Wizard Shadowmender and he nodded. I would need his support to help Kat's family disappear out of the reach of the vampires. "Yes," I replied firmly.

"That's all I need to know," Kat said, tears shining in her eyes. She reached up and began clawing at the head dress as though it was on fire. "Get this thing off me," she yelled, and I dug in gladly, seeking a way to extricate her from the repugnant cage encasing her skull. Charity rushed towards us to lend a hand too.

I cast a wary glance back to where Melchior was standing alone. Like Sabien and Gorkha on the dais, he had been encased in the elliptical energy field. I feared that one of them could leap forward and interfere, but each remained where they were, equally helpless, brimming with rage. Melchior—tensing and untensing his hands and gritting his teeth—looked as though he would like to strangle someone. Preferably me or my elderly wizard friend, I imagined.

"Have you lost your mind?" he spat at Kat. "Set me free. Let's finish this ceremony once and for all. You know I can make your life a living hell, Ekaterina."

Kat rounded on him once more. "You have *already* made my life a living hell, Melchior. For months. Ever since you met me and insisted on this faux marriage. But now my mother and my sister are safe, and they will remain protected here at this inn, thanks to Alf and Wizard Shadowmender. I don't need to marry you anymore. You have no power left—no way of lording over me. I do not give my immortal soul to you."

Charity worked the final clasp free and the heavy crown fell to the floor with a loud thunk. Kat jumped from the dais and grasped Marc's hand while our guests inched forwards, returning after running away, watching all the proceedings avidly. Kat shouted up into Melchior's furious face, "I'm free now. Free of you. I will marry the man I love. The man who loves me. Who loves me as I am and has no wish to change me. The one who would move heaven and earth to see me happy. Who would reunite me with my loved ones, not threaten their very existence. I'm going to marry Marc."

Melchior stunned by her malevolence glared firstly at her and then at me. "You put her up to this," he hissed.

"Alf had nothing to do with it." Kat jumped straight in before I could say a word. "I don't need anyone else to show me what a complete waste of space and oxygen you are, Melchior Laurent."

"You'll regret this," Melchior wagged his finger at her. "I'll make sure you do. And as for you," he glared Marc, "I'll make sure you pay. I'll have you torn limb from limb. You know I can do it." He shook his head and laughed, a deeply troubled and hollow sound. "I can't believe you'd choose this loser over me," he scowled at Kat. "He can't ever do anything right."

Marc wrapped his arm around Kat and bent

down to kiss the top of her head. Kat peered up at him, her expression soft and loving. "He's done alright by me so far," she smiled.

Five minutes later, under Wizard Shadowmender's watchful eye, a cloud of bats took to the skies above my wonky inn. I observed their departure with relief. They twisted and rolled as they passed across the moon, their movements unnatural and lacking in grace, as though operated by some hidden puppeteer.

We had moved the remaining guests inside the inn, where Charity was running a free bar, and Luppitt Smeatharpe and his friends were rocking the joint. Wizard Shadowmender had ensured a smooth departure of our unwanted fanged friends, and at the end, Sabien had yet again proved to be a calming influence on his son. When the wizard sternly but politely requested the vampires take their leave, Sabien quickly assembled his party and issued the necessary instructions.

Charming to the last, Sabien took my hand and held it to his lips. "I'm sorry it had to end like this, Alfhild."

"Me too," I lied.

"And I'm sorry for all ze trouble my son has caused. Perhaps Marc is right, and Melchior does still have a great deal of growing up to do."

I had to agree with that. "What about Kat's family?" I asked. "And Marc and Kat? Can you promise they will be safe?"

"I will attempt to make it so, but Melchior, he likes to get his own way. I will try to distract him with a new playmate, perhaps." Sabien laughed and I resisted curling my lip in repugnance. With Wizard Shadowmender's help I would ensure Kat's family remained forever out of the vampire's field of vision.

"And what about you? How will you keep yourself safe?" Sabien asked, and while he said this with a smile, I sensed the steel behind his gaze and heard the warning in his tone.

I glanced back at the inn behind me, lit up with warmth and energy, music and laughter drifting from the open windows and doors.

"Every day that I live here I derive power from the inn itself, from my land, the forest and my friends. I have all the protection I need, Sabien, and I will be forever watchful and alert. Don't think that I won't. A witch's strength is drawn from nature, and from deep within herself."

Sabien bowed his head. "In spite of everything, I am honoured to have met you, Alfhild. The hearses will return for our belongings. I will settle the bill when I return to Paris. Until we meet again." And with that, he must have passed some secret signal because as one, the vampires leapt into the sky, obscuring the stars and transforming in the blackness of the night, and with a great fluttering, sped clumsily away.

Wizard Shadowmender and I stood together and silently watched them disappear. When every single one of them were out of sight, I let out a sigh of relief.

"Better?" Wizard Shadowmender asked and I nodded.

"Much better." I smiled at him. "Thank you for showing up when you did. How did you know?"

The elderly wizard glanced back at the inn. "A little bird told me." An evasive answer I thought.

I suggested he go inside in the warm while I mooched around, switching off fairy lights and dowsing the braziers, picking up stray champagne flutes that had been discarded as the vampires took to the wing. He did so, and when I'd been around the garden once, I scanned the area for anything obvious I needed to attend to before the morning, intent on following him in.

A single red light appeared to be glowing in the hedge behind the arbour. I meandered over, figuring it was a solar light that I could do nothing about, my mind distracted and in a hurry to join the party inside. Ten feet from the light I stopped still, watching it spin, the tell-tale gold thread running through it, tiny sparks of light flying out as it gyrated, my breath catching in my throat and the familiar vein of panic stroking icy fingers down my spine.

"*Relinquo*," I commanded it. "You are not welcome here."

It hung in the air, no larger than a ping-pong ball, then backed away through the hedge, fading from view. Too close for comfort. I would have to tell Wizard Shadowmender about this and ask for his help to step up the protective circle around the inn and my grounds.

The Mori back here at Whittle Inn? It could not be countenanced.

The memory of the last time I'd seen Jed wormed its way uneasily into my mind: in the clearing at the centre of Speckled Wood. I could have used the Curse of Madb on him. I could have finished him off once and for all. Perhaps I'd been misguided.

Perhaps I had been weak.

I watched the spinning globe go, fear gripping my intestines. First Derek and now this appearance. Clearly, The Mori had not finished with me yet. Were they still after my inn, and the land it stood on?

I shivered in the cold air, goose bumps prickling along the back of my neck as I frowned into the darkness. I still had no idea what Derek Pearce's link to The Mori had been. Why had The Mori been at his house? Had they killed him? I assumed so. And why had Derek been storing chemicals in his shed at the allotments?

I needed answers.

Looking after my wonky inn felt like a daunting task at times, but I had to remember I was not doing this alone.

I turned my face to the stars, purposefully placing my back to the hedge and the orb, and walked towards the inn, trying to shake off the feeling of being watched.

Paranoia.

George was waiting for me inside. For now, it was time to party.

I plastered a carefree smile on my face and joined them—a smiling George who wrapped an arm around my waist, Charity busily serving drinks at the bar and looking supremely in control, her pretty pink hair standing on end, and all my friends from Whittlecombe including Rhona—accompanied of course by Stan who looked so much better—all singing the praises of Millicent's blackberry potion.

Marc and Kat briefly broke off from dancing to join George and I. Kat had scrubbed her face clean, then hacked most of the layers of her skirt away with a pair of blunt scissors we kept behind the bar, so now she was sporting a short and ragged version of her wedding dress, the beads still shimmying in the light. She looked magnificent.

"Thank you for all you've done, Alf," she said, hugging me tight. We had discussed how I would put the feelers out, with some assistance from Wizard Shadowmender, and find somewhere Kat's mother and sister would be safe. "You freed me from a tyrant and now I can be with the man of my dreams instead."

"I'll drink to that," I said, and we clinked champagne glasses. I wondered how Kat and Marc would make their new lives work, her as a mortal and him immortal. And would they ever stop looking over their shoulders with Melchior at large in the world? But they were special people, they would make it succeed somehow, some way.

"Do me a favour?" A sudden thought had

occurred to me. "If you ever want to get married... please don't hold the event at Whittle Inn. It's going to take me years to recover from this one."

Kat pouted. I winked, and everyone joined in laughing.

But seriously? I made a mental note to bar vampires henceforth from Whittle Inn.

Epilogue

When I awoke the next morning I had a little bit of a sore head. What's a woman to do when the champagne is running so freely, and the culmination of her dreams—the opening of Whittle Inn in my case—had finally come to fruition. Gentle tapping at my window alerted me to the arrival of Mr Hoo. I leapt out of bed, my head thumping in indignation at the sudden activity, and opened the window wide, allowing him to fly in and take his place on my bedpost.

"Where have you been?" I asked, my voice husky. "I've been so worried about you."

"Hoo-ooo. Hoo-ooo."

"Is that so? Well you've missed some adventures here, I can tell you." I reached out and gently scratched his feathery head. "I'm so pleased you're back. I really missed you, little fellow."

With only five hours sleep, after a week of hardly any sleep at all, it's safe to say I looked a little worse for wear when I made my way groggily downstairs in search of toast and tea.

And lots of it.

Florence was in the bar, beginning to clear up a scene that looked like something out of a post-apocalyptic movie. Luppitt Smeatharpe and the Devonshire Fellows were slumped over their instruments in the corner and Zephaniah was asleep under one of the buffet tables.

Who knew ghosts became tired too?

Florence smiled when she saw me. "Morning miss," she said. "You look like you need a pick me up."

"Urgh," I groaned. "You're not kidding. Has Charity surfaced yet?"

"No miss. Would you like me to wake her?"

"No let her sleep." She deserved it. She'd been working like a trojan.

I headed for the frosted glass door and the back of the inn where the kitchen was located—where the bread and butter and marmalade were located, more importantly—but Florence stopped me. "The hearses came back before dawn, Miss Alf."

I turned back. "They took all the coffins?"

"All but two."

Thaddeus and Marc. Now that the vampires had departed Whittle Inn, I supposed I'd never find out who had killed Thaddeus. There was a big question mark there. I'd have to dispose of Thaddeus's coffin myself. "And Marc?" I asked.

"Safe in the attic, miss."

I breathed out heavily, relieved all had gone to plan. We would send Marc on to Kat as soon as she had found a suitable and safe location.

Monsieur Emietter was already beavering away in his pristine kitchen. "Morning," I trilled, cheerier than I felt. "May I have some toast and tea please?"

Monsieur Emietter looked at me askance. Either he didn't even know enough English to provide me with tea and toast or he didn't want to mess up his impeccably clean and tidy worktops.

"Toast? Tea?" I tried again. "Maybe even a bacon sandwich. Or what about eggs and bacon? What's the French for eggs and bacon?"

Monsieur Emietter offered me one of his now famous gallic shrugs, his face blank.

"Maybe even throw in a sausage." I wanted to bash my head against the kitchen table. What was the use of a chef I couldn't communicate with? "But don't forget the toast."

I made a move for the breadbin myself and Monsieur Emietter made a dismissing motion at my fingers. I started to retort when I noted the glint in his eye. He was having me on.

He winked, indicated I should sit at the table, and began pulling items from the fridge and cold store. Removing the bread from the bread bin he cut a slice and shoved it in the toaster. Then turned to look at me, raising one finger, then two, then three. I laughed with delight.

Charity picked that moment to join me in the kitchen, still clad in her pyjamas. "Oh, please may I have some too?" she asked. "I need something to sop up the champagne."

"Just give us all the toast," I demanded and patted my belly, and Monsieur Emietter grinned.

A few minutes later we were squealing with delight when he handed over a dinner plate full of steaming hot toast. "I don't know where yours is," Charity said trying to take the plate off me. We giggled together until a familiar voice piped up from directly in front of us.

"Have you seen the state of the bar, Alfhild? You should be out there helping Florence tidy up."

Gwyn rapidly apparated into vision.

"There you are!" I could have hugged her, had that been possible.

"Has there been a party? What did I miss?" She affected a look of total innocence.

I shook my head. "Grandmama? You have no idea."

Jeannie Wycherley
26th December 2018

Acknowledgements

Huge thanks as always to my sensational street team, and a shout-out to my ARC readers over on Booksprout who have been so effusive and supportive as regards the Wonky Inn Books. I have been completely taken aback by the love I've had for Alf and her friends.

Special thanks to JC Clarke of The Graphics Shed for her phenomenal covers, and to Anna Bloom once more, for her sensible suggestions and common-sense approach, her passion and her belief.

To my husband John for his love and support, and my friends, real and virtual, who cheer me on when the going gets tough.

Finally, most importantly, thanks to you, the reader. I

love bringing you my stories, reading your reviews, and receiving your feedback. You complete my circle.

Much love 🖤

Jeannie Wycherley
Devon, UK
28th November 2018

Wonky Continues

Fearful Fortunes and Terrible Tarot: Wonky Inn Book 4

There's a psychic fayre heading to Whittlecombe.

Alf, the witch, didn't see it coming … perhaps she should have done.

Whittle Inn is up and running and gaining in popularity. Proud owner Alfhild Daemonne can afford to relax, can't she?

Apparently not.

When her neighbouring inn decides to host the south west region's largest ever Psychic and Holistic

Convention, you'd think that would allow Alf the opportunity to make lots of new friends. Think of it! Dozens and dozens of fortune tellers, mediums, diviners, psychics, rune-tellers, witch doctors, and even a voodoo priestess from New Orleans – all gathered together in one big field.

Not so.

Alf is banned from attending the Fayre and looks set to miss out - until Wizard Shadowmender sends her on an undercover operation that is.

In the meantime, someone is sending Alf death threats and many of her friends in the village of Whittlecombe are subject to fearful fortune tellings and terrible tarot readings at the Fayre.

It appears that dark forces are gathering in Whittlecombe.

Will Alf make it to her 31st birthday?

And just who is it that wishes her harm?

Find out when you read Wonky Inn Book 4 today.

ADD SOME MAGICKAL SPARKLE

Add some magickal sparkle to your Christmas with a Christmas Wonky Novella

The Witch Who Killed Christmas

It's an ill wind that blows no good...

An unexpected snowmageddon threatens to derail Christmas at Alfhild Daemonne's inn.

She's hosting her first festive celebration, so she's understandably disappointed when guests begin cancelling bookings, thanks to the abnormal wintery conditions in the south west of England.

When Alf receives information that there may be an ulterior reason for the weather anomaly, she journeys deep into the forest in search of a witch with an attitude problem.

Can Alf save Christmas at Wonky Inn? Or will one mean old witch kill Christmas for everyone?

The Witch Who Killed Christmas can be read as a standalone or as part of the Wonky Inn series.

THE BIRTH OF WONKY

In Case You Missed the Birth of Wonky

The story begins...

The Wonkiest Witch: Wonky Inn Book 1

Alfhild Daemonne has inherited an inn.
and a dead body.

Estranged from her witch mother, and having committed to little in her thirty years, Alf surprises herself when she decides to start a new life.

She heads deep into the English countryside intent on making a success of the once popular inn. However, discovering the murder throws her a curve ball. Especially when she suspects dark magick.

Additionally, a less than warm welcome from several locals, persuades her that a variety of folk – of both the mortal and magickal persuasions – have it in for her.

The dilapidated inn presents a huge challenge for Alf. Uncertain who to trust, she considers calling time on the venture.

Should she pack her bags and head back to London? Don't be daft.

Alf's magickal powers may be as wonky as the inn, but she's dead set on finding the murderer.

Once a witch always a witch, and this one is fighting back.
A clean and cozy witch mystery.

Take the opportunity to immerse yourself in this fantastic new witch mystery series, from the author of the award-winning novel, Crone.

Grab Book 1 of the Wonky Inn series, The Wonkiest Witch, right here

PLEASE?

Please consider leaving a review?

If you have enjoyed reading The Witch Who Killed Christmas, please consider leaving me a review.

Reviews help to spread the word about my writing, which takes me a step closer to my dream of writing full time.

If you are kind enough to leave a review, please also consider joining my Author Street Team on Facebook – Jeannie Wycherley's Fiendish Street Team. Do let me know you left a review when you apply because it's a closed group. You can find my fiendish team at

PLEASE?

https://www.facebook.com/groups/JeannieWycherleysFiends/

You'll have the chance to Beta read and get your hands on advanced review eBook copies from time to time. I also appreciate your input when I need some help with covers, blurbs etc.

Or sign up for my newsletter http://eepurl.com/cN3Q6L to keep up to date with what I'm doing next!

THE WONKY INN SERIES

The Wonky Inn Series

The Wonkiest Witch: Wonky Inn Book 1
The Ghosts of Wonky Inn: Wonky Inn Book 2
Weird Wedding: Wonky Inn Book 3
Fearful Fortunes and Terrible Tarot: Wonky Inn Book 4 Due for release 31st January 2019
The Mystery of the Marsh Malaise: Wonky Inn Book 5 Due for release March 2019
The Witch Who Killed Christmas: Wonky Inn Christmas Special

Also By

Beyond the Veil (2018)

Crone (2017)

A Concerto for the Dead and Dying (short story, 2018)

Deadly Encounters: A collection of short stories (2017)

Keepers of the Flame: A love story (Novella, 2018)

Non Fiction

Losing my best Friend Thoughtful support for those affected by dog bereavement or pet loss (2017)

Follow Jeannie Wycherley

Find out more at on the website
www.jeanniewycherley.co.uk

You can tweet Jeannie twitter.com/Thecushionlady

Or visit her on Facebook for her fiction

www.facebook.com/jeanniewycherley

Sign up for Jeannie's newsletter
http://eepurl.com/cN3Q6L

COMING SOON

The Municipality of Lost Souls by Jeannie Wycherley

Described as a cross between Daphne Du Maurier's *Jamaica Inn*, and TV's *The Walking Dead*, but with ghosts instead of zombies, *The Municipality of Lost Souls* tells the story of Amelia Fliss and her cousin Agatha Wick.

In the otherwise quiet municipality of Durscombe, the inhabitants of the small seaside town harbour a deadly secret.

Amelia Fliss, wife of a wealthy merchant, is the lone voice who speaks out against the deadly practice of the wrecking and plundering of ships on the rocks in Lyme bay, but no-one appears to be listening to her.

As evil and malcontent spread like cholera throughout the community, and the locals point fingers and vow to take vengeance against outsiders, the dead take it upon themselves to end a barbaric tradition the living seem to lack the will to stop.

Set in Devon in the UK during the 1860s, *The Municipality of Lost Souls* is a Victorian Gothic ghost story, with characters who will leave their mark on you forever.

If you enjoyed *Beyond the Veil*, you really don't want to miss this novel.

Sign up for my newsletter or join my Facebook group today.

Printed in Great Britain
by Amazon